Outrageously Yours

OUTRAGEOUSLY YOURS

BRUCE WEST

A PERIGEE BOOK

Perigee Books
are published by
The Putnam Publishing Group
200 Madison Avenue
New York, NY 10016

Library of Congress Cataloging-in-Publication Data
West, Bruce, date.
Outrageously yours.

1. Canadian wit and humor. 2. Celebrities—
Correspondence. 3. Canadian letters. I. Title.
PN6178.C3W47   1987   808.88   87-7315
ISBN 0-399-51410-4 (pbk.)

Typeset by Fisher Composition, Inc.

Published by arrangement with Stoddart Publishing Co. Limited

Printed in the United States of America
1   2   3   4   5   6   7   8   9   10

The author, a trainee construction laborer who resides in a sleepy seaside retirement town on the edge of nowhere, has selflessly assumed the daunting burden of establishing a vital link between the ordinary person and People of Consequence who exercise their influence on our everyday lives.

The Town Hall   104-1037 West Broadway
Carmel-by-the-Sea   Vancouver
California 93921   British Columbia
U.S.A.   Canada V6H 1E3

For the attention of His Honor   June 3 1987
Mayor Clint Eastwood

Your Honor,

    Or may we still call you Clint‼ I've seen all your movies of course,
some of them several times, and I'm sure your millions of fans all over the
world were deeply moved by your appointment as mayor of Carmel, and share my
profound relief that you have finally abandoned all hope of becoming an actor‼

    You've been mayor for over a year now, Clint, and I wonder if this
elevation has inspired you to yet greater ambition, as one doubts that the
legendary economy of dialogue for which you are deservedly infamous, can be
relied upon to precipitate an avalanche of invitations to professorial
ordination with any of the country's discerning seats of education‼
No matter, I'm sure you are an excellent mayor, and I'm delighted to tell
you that my family and I will be driving down to visit your town next month‼
Actually it will just be myself with Uncle Jasper and old Aunt Griselda, who
claims to be in her mid-eighties, but I'm sure she's considerably older than
she admits‼ I don't drive myself, and Uncle's no longer licensed since the
recent judicial misunderstanding where he severely damaged the Judge's
bicycle with his combine harvester, so Aunt Griselda will be handling the
transportation‼

    To be honest, Your Honor, my Aunt is not keen on driving in Carmel,
as she is getting pretty decrepit these days, and her eyesight is so poor
she is barely able to see, particularly when finding somewhere to stop, as
she cannot read 'No Parking' signs to save her life‼ Not that there is a
problem paying the parking tickets, she's not short of money by any means.
No, the fact is, she has also seen all your old movies, which at her advanced
years she tends to take rather literally, and she's terrified that if you
catch her parking illegally, you'll charge at her with steely glint, resolute
jaw, six-shooter blazing from the hip, and ask questions afterwards‼
At her age, Clint, she tends to be allergic to multiple bullet wounds and
severe physical beatings, and they could also disagree with her prescribed
medications.

    So, to allay her fears and make what will hopefully be her last
vacation thoroughly memorable, I wonder if you could use your influence to
issue a special Parking Exemption Permit for my dear old Aunt? We'd all be
very relieved if you could help keep the old broad out of trouble, and if
you would also be kind enough to send an autographed photo of you in your
official mayoral habergeon, that would be a real bonus‼

    I enclose five dollars to cover the Permit and photo, please let me
know if this is not enough, and I will remit the balance by return.

    Go ahead, Mayor, make Aunt Griselda's day‼

    Thanks, Clint‼‼

                                           Yours sincerely,

Enc.   Bruce West

19 June 1987

Mr. Bruce West
104-1037 West Broadway
Vancouver British Columbia
Canada   V6H 1E3

Dear Mr. West,

Sorry, no special parking permits available for
Aunt Griselda, photo enclosed.

Best,

Clint Eastwood,
Mayor

CE/tlt
Enclosure

309-941 West 13th Avenue
Vancouver
British Columbia
Canada V5Z 1P4

American Express Co.
American Express Plaza
New York
N.Y.10004
U.S.A.

August 30th 1984

For the attention of James D. Robinson 111
Chairman

Dear Mr. Robinson,

    I am sure that I speak for the vast majority of television
viewers when I congratulate your Company on the refreshingly honest
advertising campaign currently being broadcast to our homes.

    I refer of course to your employment of the putty nosed
belligerent late of 'Streets of San Francisco', who reminds us of
the dangers of travelling abroad with American Express Travellers
Cheques.

    I am myself about to embark upon an extensive foray to
foreign parts, and am naturally extremely alarmed that your cheques
are subject to such epidemic proportions of widespread larceny.
I have a busy touring schedule, and can ill afford time spent in
some frightful vermin infested foreign police station, having ones
sensibilities sorely tried by a lethargic garlic breathing policeman,
as one attempts to extract directions to one of your good offices
to report a felony.

    In the circumstances of your public spiritedness therefore,
I wonder if you might recommend a more suitable form of currency,
which could be carried with a modicum of confidence that one might
be more able to safely retain same until the conclusion of ones
travels.

    Thank you in anticipation.

Yours sincerely,

Bruce West

JAMES F. CALVANO
PRESIDENT
PAYMENT SYSTEMS DIVISION

September 21, 1984

Dear Mr. West:

Thank you for writing to Mr. Robinson recently. Your
letter was referred to me as it relates to an area of my
responsibility.

Your comments concerning our advertising program are
certainly appreciated. Our marketing efforts to alert
consumers to our unique financial products and services
have proven highly successful.

We believe American Express Travelers Cheques are the
safest and most convenient means of payment for pur-
chases when traveling away from home. No other payment
instrument provides special refund services should a
traveler become a victim of theft. You may have our
assurance that adequate security measures are continually
enforced to help protect all parties from fraudulent use.

For your travel convenience, I've enclosed a copy of our
latest <u>Traveler's Companion</u>, which I am sure you will find
useful when vacationing. The directory contains a listing
of offices of the worldwide Travel Service Network as well
as helpful suggestions.

Thank you again for taking the time and trouble to write.
The confidence our Members place in us continues to be
among our greatest assets.

Sincerely,

J. F. Calvano

Mr. Bruce West
309-941 West 13th Avenue
Vancouver
British Columbia
Canada V5Z 1P4

Enclosure

309-941 West 13th Avenue
Vancouver
British Columbia
Canada V5Z 1P4

American Express Co.
American Express Plaza
New York
N.Y.10004
U.S.A.

October 3rd 1984

For the attention of Sanford I. Weill
<u>President</u>

Dear Mr. Weill,

What on earth's happening?

I wrote to your Chairman, James D. Robinson lll on
August 30th, expressing my admiration of your current advertising
on the television, requesting at the same time his advice on
matters with which you people seem most cognizant, and to date I
have heard nothing.

Surely the very life-blood of an effective advertising
campaign is fluid communication with the target audience?

I'm a simple self made man, like yourself no doubt, and
I certainly wouldn't have got where I am today by allowing my
correspondence to gather dust whilst I was diverted elsewhere with
my personal secretary.

Perhaps you could look into this for me Sanford, and put
a squib up the Robinson fellow over his tardy performance.

Yours sincerely,

Bruce West

AMERICAN EXPRESS COMPANY
AMERICAN EXPRESS PLAZA, NEW YORK, N.Y. 10004

EXECUTIVE OFFICES

October 10, 1984

Dear Mr. West:

Enclosed is a copy of Mr. Robinson's reply to your
letter of August 30, which you should have received
by now.

Don't hesitate to contact us again should you wish,
but I would appreciate your being a bit more polite
the next time.

Sincerely,

Valerie A. La Sala
Assistant to Mr. Weill

Bruce West
309-941 West 13th Avenue
Vancouver
British Columbia
Canada V5Z 1P4

309-941 West 13th Avenue
Vancouver
British Columbia
Canada V5Z 1P4

American Express Company   October 23rd 1984
American Express Plaza
New York
N.Y.10004
U.S.A.

For the attention of Valerie A. La Sala
Assistant to Mr. Weill

Dear Valerie,

        I don't understand. I was being polite.

                        Yours sincerely,

                        Bruce West

309-941 West 13th Avenue
Vancouver
British Columbia
V5Z 1P4

Geoffrey Stevens
Managing Editor
The Globe & Mail
444 Front Street W.   September 7th 1984
Toronto
Ontario M5V 2S9

Dear Mr. Stevens,

        I write as a concerned political analyst regarding the
book review in the Globe & Mail (August 25th page E8) wherein
Jeffrey Simpson states that Prime Minister John Turner is a
committed Catholic who at one stage considered priesthood.

        No doubt you would agree with me that a man's <u>private</u>
religious persuasion is his own business, however extreme or bizarre
it may appear. The Canadian voting public however, cannot be
assumed to be as broad minded as you and I, and I must state
therefore that I think the publishing of this review during
Mr. Turner's campaign is grossly irresponsible.

        I note incidentally that no such potentially damaging
reviews on the lives of Mr. Mulroney or Mr. Broadbent were
carried by the Globe during the election campaign, to balance
any influence on the electorate.

        I have kept in close personal contact with Mr. Turner
throughout his campaign, and I know that although he is not the
sort of man to demand a satisfactory explanation from your paper,
there is no doubt that a written apology would be the least one
could expect in the circumstances.

        I await sir, your immediate reply.

                                Yours sincerely,

                                Bruce West

The Globe and Mail

OFFICE OF THE
MANAGING EDITOR

444 FRONT STREET WEST
TORONTO, M5V 2S9

September 21, 1984

Bruce West
309-941 West 13th Avenue
Vancouver, B.C.
V5Z 1P4

My Dear Mr. West:

Your letter of 7 September could scarcely have been
more to the point. I concur wholeheartedley with
your assessment of the receptivity of the masses.
The public is not - and could not reasonably be
expected to be - as broad-minded as you and I when
it comes to accepting the bizarre private religious
convictions of our leaders.

Jeffrey Simpson did state that John Turner is a
committed Catholic who once considered entering the
priesthood. I have scoured the files. I have searched
every nook and cranny of the computer, but I can find
no equivalent attack on any politician of the Progressive
Conservative or even New Democratic party stripe. In
neither of those parties did we uncover (I suspect we
may not even have endeavored to uncover) a single
Anabaptist or Zoroastrian. Who knows how many Swabians,
let alone zooflagellates, may be lurking in the
corridors of our new Government.

Your reprimand is well taken. I trust you will show
the same commendable dispatch in drawing any future
lapses to my attention.

I am,

Your Ob't Servant,

Geoffrey Stevens

/ss

309-941 West 13th Avenue
Vancouver
British Columbia
V5Z 1P4

The Globe & Mail
444 Front Street West
Toronto
Ontario
M5V 2S9

September 29th 1984

For the attention of Geoffrey Stevens
Managing Editor

Dear Mr. Stevens,

I am deeply moved by your letter dated September 21st,
not only because it serves as a profound testimonial to the
ultimate dedication one expects of a Leader of the Free Press,
but because outside our respective professional obligations we
both strive toward the common goal of a political machine free
from obsolete doctrinarianism.

Your sober approbation of one's concern over the doubtful
elements infiltrating the corridors of power in this fair country
inspires one to a renewed sense of patriotism.

You may rest assured that my people at this end will be
maintaining a critical watch on matters political as you suggest,
and any sightings of Muggletonian, Druid, Christadelphian, Jansenist,
or like convocation, will be immediately forwarded to your good
office for expert analysis.

Yours gratefully

Bruce West

309-941 West 13th Avenue
Vancouver
British Columbia
V5Z 1P4

Brian Mulroney
Progressive Conservative Party
House of Commons
OTTAWA
Ontario K1A 0A2   August 23rd 1984

Dear Mr. Mulroney,

If the polls are to be relied upon, it would appear likely
that our next government will be formed by your Party.

In the past, I have normally favoured the Liberals as being
fairly sound people, but with the departure of Mr. Trudeau, I feel
sure that their path to obscurity will be swift under the lack-lustre
'leadership' of the appalling John Turner.

Thus, I am bound to say that providing you are able to
satisfy me regarding a couple of issues, the Progressive Conservatives
may count upon my enthusiastic support in the future.

I have seen your performance on the television and in the
newspapers Mr. Mulroney, and there is no doubt that you are an
eloquent speaker, sharp, positive, and forthright - well done!

However, I should very much like you to make your position
quite clear regarding Conservative policy toward Ronald Reagan, the
ex-film star and now U.S.A. President.

Those of us who are heavily committed to psychological
research are in little doubt that Mr. Reagan is a megalomaniac,
intent on early destruction of all countries in the Eastern Bloc.

Like yourself, Mr. Reagan is of Irish origin, not necessarily
a hindrance in itself - a man cannot be held responsible for his
ethnic origins, but I have spent some time in Ireland studying the
people, and it is abundantly clear that the native physiology lacks
certain attributes that one would consider essential in responsible
political leadership.

If elected next month, I should also like assurances that you
will not emulate the policies of your counterparts in Britain, where
the Pound Sterling is at an all time low, and unemployment is at an
all time high.

My allegiance to the Progressive Conservatives will hinge on
your satisfactory comment regarding these points.

I look forward to hearing from you.

Yours sincerely,

Bruce West

CANADA

PRIME MINISTER • PREMIER MINISTRE

Ottawa, K1A 0A2
September 27, 1984

Mr. Bruce West,
Apartment 309,
941 West 13th Avenue,
Vancouver, British Columbia.
V5Z 1P4

Dear Mr. West,

      I wish to acknowledge and thank you for your letter of August 23.

      The people of Canada voted in a decisive manner for our Party because they had confidence in the ability of my colleagues and me to govern effectively and responsibly. We take seriously the mandate given to us by the electorate and I can assure you we will act in Canada's best interests at all times.

      Again, I appreciate your writing and I hope you will keep me informed of your views in the months ahead.

      With every good wish,

      Yours sincerely,

309-941 West 13th Avenue
Vancouver
British Columbia
Canada V5Z 1P4

President Ronald Reagan
The White House
Washington D.C.
20500
U.S.A.

September 6th 1984

Dear Mr. Reagan,

     Turn the other cheek to the woolly minded leftist
liberals who jump down your throat at the merest jocular threat
to bomb the Russians. I speak for a large majority of clear
thinking Canadians when I affirm our support of your commendable
policy that all communist aggressors should be wiped off the face
of the Earth, in spite of the extreme likelihood of terminal
global annihilation.

     More power to your elbow; North America and the Free World
waits with bated breath for your next inspired gem of unparalleled
diplomatic genius.

     By now of course, you will be aware that Brian Mulroney
(I believe you have already exchanged pleasantries) is to be our
next Prime Minister. I feel sure that you will get on well with
Mr. Mulroney, who in these early stages is obviously not a Great
Leader like yourself, but he shapes up well.

     It would be an exaggeration for me to claim to be close
to Mr. Mulroney, but we do exchange private correspondence from
time to time on various matters of National importance, and I can
commend him to you most highly, in spite of his relative inexperience.

     May I take this opportunity to wish you well in your
personal election campaign, and if at any time I can assist you to
your just deserts, I am at your service!

Yours sincerely,

Bruce West

309-941 West 13th Avenue
Vancouver
British Columbia
V5Z 1P4

Brian Mulroney
Progressive Conservative Party
House of Commons
OTTAWA
Ontario K1A 0A2

September 6th 1984

Dear Mr. Mulroney,

Many congratulations on the Tory landslide, due in no small part to your eloquent speech writers and omnipresent wife, Mila.

Cynics among us may claim the lack of opposition offered by the retarded performance of Mr. Turner, and the blustering Mr. Broadbent (NDP), made for an easy victory, but I for one am not unimpressed by the outcome, and anticipate early adherence to all the Progressive Conservative promises.

I have incidentally, recently enjoyed an exchange of private letters with the American President, Ronald Reagan, and have in the course of same, reassured him as to your suitability for the leadership of this great country.

I do hope that my assurances to the President will stand the test of time.

If I can be of further service, I am at your command.

Yours sincerely,

Bruce West

CANADA

PRIME MINISTER · PREMIER MINISTRE

Ottawa, K1A 0A2
November 9, 1984

Dear Bruce,

    I would like to thank you so much for your very kind words of congratulations and best wishes on our Party's victory in the recent election. I was delighted to receive your letter.

    The overwhelming mandate which the Canadian people gave us on September 4 is a responsibility we will treat with care and dignity. Our new government will immediately set to work to restore prosperity and opportunity to this great country in full recognition of the tremendous encouragement we have so recently received from the people of Canada.

    The work, effort and convictions of a great many people were necessary to make this victory possible. These next few months will be a challenging time for us as we begin to establish the government which Progressive Conservatives across this country have worked so hard to make happen.

    Thank you again for your letter. It was a pleasure to hear from you.

    With every good wish,

                    Yours sincerely,

                    Brian Mulroney

Mr. Bruce West,
    Apartment 309,
        941 West 13th Avenue,
            Vancouver, British Columbia.
                V5Z 1P4

309-941 West 13th Avenue
Vancouver
British Columbia
Canada V5Z 1P4

President Ronald Reagan
The White House
Washington D.C.
U.S.A.
20500

October 10th 1984

Dear Mr. Reagan,

I am both shocked and disappointed!

I wrote to you on September 6th expressing my admiration for your courageous approach to the severe global problems confronting the civilised peoples of our two great countries, also putting to paper my wishes for your sempiternal and cordial rapport with Brian Mulroney, and to date I have not received the common courtesy of a reply.

Is this the American way?

If we are to maintain a policy of improving relations, then surely our mutual obligations must include fluid communication.

I have on my desk a letter from Mr. Mulroney, dated September 27th, concerning various matters of state, in which he also requests of me, "I hope you will keep me informed of your views in the months ahead", and to this end I should certainly wish to be able to include a line of encouragement concerning the combined efforts of our two nations to at least demonstrate the ability to enjoy a respectful interchange of letters.

I know that you in particular Mr. President, as an equilibrist and Christian, personally deplore laxity of behaviour in social intercourse, and I am assuming therefore that your failure to reply to my letter is an isolated oversight.

I trust I may now look forward to your early missive.

Yours sincerely,

Bruce West

Note: No reply received. —Ed.

309-941 West 13th Avenue
Vancouver
British Columbia
Canada V5Z 1P4

Jimmy Carter
75 Spring Street
Atlanta
Georgia 30303
U.S.A.

December 15th 1984

Dear Jimmy,

     I expect you were as disappointed as I was last month,
with the re-election of the ex-film star Ronald Reagan as
President of the United States for another four years.

     To a man like yourself, possessed of superior intellect
and razor-sharp wit, it must be particularly galling to suffer
a President of whom it has been said is a complete imbecile
when it comes to operating without a vast team of advisers to
keep him out of trouble?

     No Sir, it was a sad loss to international politics
when we saw the last of your cheery bovine grin in harmony with
your spellbinding articulation and sharp delivery, demonstrating
to us all that no matter what else, America was still America!

     As a permanent reminder to me that you really were once
the President of the United States, I wonder if I could ask for
an autographed photo of you to take pride of place in my modest
Gallery of Great Statesmen?

     I enclose a dollar to cover postage, and thank you kindly
in anticipation.

                                        Yours respectfully,

                                        Bruce West

Enc.

With Best Wishes,

Jimmy Carter

```
                                                      309-941 West 13th Avenue
                                                      Vancouver
                                                      British Columbia
Canadian Conference of Catholic Bishops               V5Z 1P4
90 Parent Avenue
Ottawa
Ontario K1N 7B1                                       October 22nd 1984
```

For the attention of Most Reverend John Sherlock

Dear Most Reverend Father,

My conscience directs my hand to beg your guidance over a deeply distressing incident which has been my recent experience.

I was proceeding about my lawful occasion down a main street late one evening, when my attention was engaged by a young lady whose attire was startling to say the least, particularly in view of the cold weather. She seemed friendly enough however, and being new to this country I was pleased to stop for a chat.

Then to my horror, it suddenly dawned on me that I was being propositioned by a lady of questionable morals, and panic stricken, I fled without further ado.

My lord, did I act correctly? Was it right to have forsaken the wretched Jezebel without taking corrective action? On reflection perhaps I should have invited her to my modest garret and instructed her as to the error of her sinful ways. Or should I have assumed the more severe alternative and summoned a constable to despatch her to the cells for a sound flogging by the duty officer?

I am unfamiliar with the modern ways of the people of this country, and unsure as to the permitted code of behaviour.

Should a repetition of an incident of this type befall me in the future, what is the course of action which should be adopted?

I await your wise counsel, and apologise for troubling you over this distasteful incident.

                                          Yours sincerely,

                                          Bruce West

Copies to: John Crosbie, Attorney General.
           Commander R. H. Simmonds, R.C.M.P.

Canadian Conference of Catholic Bishops
Conférence des évêques catholiques du Canada

November 5, 1984

Mr. Bruce West
309-941 West 13th Avenue
Vancouver, B.C.
V5Z 1P4

Dear Mr. West:

Bishop John Sherlock, the President of the CCCB, shared your confidential letter with me and asked me to answer on his behalf.

From your letter, I would surmise you would wish to have more than a short answer - and an answer which could respect the seriousness and delicacy evident in your question.

For this reason, I would suggest that you consider contacting a priest in Vancouver and discuss your questions fully with him. I hope that this will provide the assistance which you seek.

Trusting this is of help.

Sincerely,

(Msgr.) Dennis J. Murphy
General Secretary

309-941 West 13th Avenue
Vancouver
British Columbia
Canada V5Z 1P4

Jehovah's Witnesses
Watchtower Society
25 Columbia Heights
Brooklyn
N.Y.11201
U.S.A.

October 27th 1984

For the attention of Frederick W. Franz
<u>President</u>

Dear Mr. Franz,

     I am sure I speak for all Witnesses when I inform
you of the shock and distress I experienced when I read in
today's 'Globe & Mail' that "Jesus Christ has returned to
earth in the form of pop superstar Michael Jackson".

     On the flimsy premise that Ms. Jackson was able to
survive a minor piloseous conflagration whilst participating
in a television commercial, must this mean we are now obliged
to brace ourselves for a new and modern image for Jehovah's
Witness theology?

     Will the excellent publication 'Watch Tower' now be
filled with glamorous show-business celebrities, hit parade
news, and advertising for pop concerts, handed to us in the
streets by drug-crazed hippies with beards down to their knees
and brains short-circuited by the ubiquitous Sony Walkman?

     I await your immediate explanation.

Yours sincerely,

Bruce West

309-941 West 13th Avenue
Vancouver
British Columbia
Canada V5Z 1P4

Jehovah's Witnesses
Watchtower Society
25 Columbia Heights
Brooklyn
N.Y.11201
U.S.A.

January 9th 1985

For the attention of Frederick W. Franz
President

Dear Mr. Franz,

I fail to understand?

I wrote to you on October 27th requesting an explanation of the sinister relationship between Jehovah's Witnesses and the omnipresent pop star Michael Jackson, and I have not been afforded the common courtesy of a reply!

Has the world as we know it gone completely mad?

As I have yet to hear of a religious order that was immune to encouragement of the financial variety, I enclose a dollar to expedite your immediate clarification of this most urgent theological dilemma.

Yours sincerely,

Bruce West

Enc.

CAMBIE CONGREGATION OF
JEHOVAH'S WITNESSES
1015 West 8th Ave
Vancouver, B.C.

March 15, 1985

Mr.Bruce West
309 - 941 West 13th Ave
Vancouver, B.C.

Dear Mr. West

     Your letter of 9th January 1985 has been received and
forwarded to us, so that we may be able to discuss with you the questions
you have presented in your letter.

     On Saturday March 9th 1985, two of our representatives called
at your home, and again later that same day phoned you. We did this because
we thought it would be a better way to deal with your proposed questions
if someone came and discussed them with you personally. You were unable
to speak with us at that time.

     If you are agreeable to this, then please feel free to call
any one of the three representatives whose phone numbers you will find
below.

     We are respectfully returning your cheque assuring you that it
was not necessary in order to get a reponse from us.

                  Yours Respectfully,

                  CAMBIE CONGREGATION OF
                  JEHOVAH'S WITNESSES

Harry Sewell   731 8437

Al Hamacher   733 8069

Brian Swire   731 2623

Enclosure: Cheque # 135: $1.00

309-941 West 13th Avenue
Vancouver
British Columbia
Canada V5Z 1P4

Elite Model Management Corp.
150 E. 58th Avenue
New York
N.Y. 10155
U.S.A.

November 20th 1984

For the attention of John Casablancas

Dear John,

It is my pleasant responsibility to be charged with organising my Rowing Club Old Boys annual get-together on Friday December 21st at a top downtown Toronto hotel.

There will be fifteen of us in all, and to complete the occasion we need an equal number of 'models' for the evening. The girls will be flown to the hotel at our expense on the Friday afternoon, and returned the following morning, again all expenses covered.

We are all wealthy businessmen, so money is no obstacle, and I need hardly mention the girls will also be well catered for in the food and drink department!

Perhaps you could initially send details and photographs of a selection of your best types, together with an indication of the total cost, and I will send a cheque by return of post.

I look forward to doing business with you.

Yours sincerely,

Bruce West

309-941 West 13th Avenue
Vancouver
British Columbia
Canada V5Z 1P4

Elite Model Management Corp.
150 E. 58th Avenue
New York
N.Y. 10155
U.S.A.

December 10th 1984

<u>For the attention of John Casablancas</u>

Dear John,

      Further to my letter of November 20th, our Rowing Club
Old Boys annual dinner has had to be postponed until Saturday
February 2nd next year, as we were unable to secure accommodation
in an hotel appropriate to the status of the occasion on the
proposed date of December 21st.

      The downtown Toronto location has not changed however,
and I trust this new date will be satisfactory to your girls?

      I enclose a deposit of two dollars, and look forward to
receiving details of our order by return post.

      Many thanks in anticipation.

Yours sincerely,

Bruce West

Enc.

elite Elite Model Management Corporation/John Casablancas

January 3, 1985

Mr. Bruce West
309-941 West 13th Avenue
Vancouver
British Columbia
Canada V5Z 1P4

Dear Mr. West:

Please find enclosed your check dated December 12th in the
amount of $2.00.

Unfortunately, Elite will not be able to participate in your
annual dinner promotion, and I am therefore returning your
check.

Very truly yours,

Loretta Wojcik
Secretary to Mr. Casablancas

JC/lw

enc.

309-941 West 13th Avenue
Vancouver
British Columbia
Canada V5Z 1P4

Gina Lollobrigida
Via Appino Antica 223
Rome
ITALY

December 1st 1984

Dear Gina,

        Through no fault of our own, my companion and I were
obliged to endure an episode of the appalling soap 'Falcon
Crest' last night.

        My shocked companion wondered why an actress of your
beauty and talent has to risk her reputation by starring in
a series geared to appeal to the undemanding and indiscriminate
North American 'intellect'?

        In bewilderment, I could only reply that as the programme
is so awful no-one would be watching it anyway, thus your
reputation would emerge unscathed!

        One appreciates that no matter how accomplished an actress
may be, the older broad does not receive the number of offers that
were enjoyed in her youth, but one would like to see the line drawn
somewhere, and in your case Gina I sincerely hope that 'Falcon
Crest' is an isolated example of professional lapse on your part.

        Here's a dollar! From a fan who would like it used to
start a fund to ensure that financial difficulties never again
force you to accept work of a standard below that which you deserve.

        With all best wishes.

                                Yours sincerely,

                                Bruce West

Enc.

309-941 West 13th Avenue
Vancouver
British Columbia
Canada V5Z 1P4

Ayatollah Ruhollah Khomeini
State Offices
Tehran
<u>IRAN</u>

January 4th 1986

Your Excellency,

    I imagine by now you must be thoroughly fed up with reading about and listening to short-sighted criticism of your monotheistic dictatorship since the departure of the late Shah of Iran?

    When I was attending College some years back, it was my privilege to study with a considerable number of students from Iran, and if I may say so, I always found them to be most pugilistic and unsavoury in every regard!

    In my humble opinion therefore, I cannot agree with world condemnation of the wholesale execution of those found guilty of serious crime in your fair country, as I have yet to meet one of your fellow countrymen undeserving of suitable peremptory correction!

    On the contrary, a simple people such as yours benefits from and indeed needs sound leadership from a lucid and compassionate ruler of your eminence!

    May I therefore extend a warm hand of international friendship to you in your hours of turbulence, and request a signed photo of Your Excellency in your splendid Official Regalia to take pride of place in my modest gallery of benevolent Conservatives?

Yours respectfully,

Bruce West

309-941 West 13th Avenue
Vancouver
British Columbia
Canada V5Z 1P4

Ayatollah Ruhollah Khomeini
State Offices
Tehran
IRAN

February 19th 1986

Your Excellency,

What's the post like in your neck of the woods?

My humble request of January 4th for a photograph
of your Highness to adorn my Gallery of Great Statesmen
has yet to bear fruit!

One assumes that you keep a few snaps handy to
amuse your few admirers - of course I could always pop
over personally with my Kodak but I expect you are far
too busy with internal executions and the like to pose
for me!

I enclose two dollars to pay for your development
costs, and look forward to receiving my photograph in early
course!

God bless you!

Yours in Admiration,

Bruce West

Enc.

Bruce West
309-941 West 13th Ave
Vancouver British
Columbia Canada
V5Z - 1P4
2VA/
Pess

BY AIR MAIL
PAR AVION

309-941 West 13th Avenue
Vancouver
British Columbia
V5Z 1P4

Molson Ontario Breweries Ltd
640 Fleet Street West
Toronto
Ontario
M5V 1B2

December 22nd 1984

For the attention of D. A. Barbour
President

Dear Mr. Barbour,

My new restaurant opens its doors for business at the beginning of February next year, and I have therefore been obliged to sample the various beers available on the market in order to decide which brands to stock.

I think I can safely claim to have a discerning palate, and I am disappointed to report that they all taste the same to me, bland, characterless, and uncomfortably gaseous. However, in spite of the lack of positive incentive from any of the varieties sampled, I have decided to stock Molson, on the assumption that your advertising is probably best geared to induce the mugs to resort to your particular beverages.

It has always seemed to me to be an unfortunate irony that social and legislative pressure dictates that alcoholic drink advertising obliges breweries to concoct subtle scenes of pleasant sporting activities, up-market social gatherings, and similar views of pretty women and well-off men, when probably one would be making a far more accurate and effective advert by coming straight to the point with, for instance, "O.K. guys, so it tastes as though it's been re-cycled through an Algerian donkey a couple of times, but if you drink it cold enough you can't taste it anyway, and at least you can get pissed on it which is what it's all about!"

Ah well, such is life.

I should incidentally like to extend an invitation to you to attend the opening of the Restaurant next February, and perhaps even to make a small speech to the assembled Press and local Dignitarys. Perhaps you might pencil this in your diary, and I will contact you with further details next month?

Yours sincerely,

Bruce West

MOLSON

OFFICE OF THE PRESIDENT

January 4, 1985.

Mr. Bruce West,
309 - 941 West 13th Avenue,
Vancouver, B.C.
V5Z 1P4

Dear Mr. West:

Thank you for your letter. I have referred it to Mr. Jack Beach,
President, Molson Brewery B.C. Ltd.

I am somewhat puzzled by your remarks about beer in general as well
as your suggested advertising copy. Surely you cannot be serious!

I trust that, if you decide to sell our products, we will have some
assurances that they will be presented in a positive manner to your
customers. Canadian beer, and Molson brands in particular, are of
the finest in the world. We would not want them represented in any
other way.

Yours sincerely,

David A. Barbour
President

cc. N. M. Seagram
     J. G. Beach

MOLSON ONTARIO BREWERIES LIMITED
640 Fleet Street, Toronto, Ontario M5V 1B2, Tel. (416) 869-1786, Telex 06218289

4625 John Street
Vancouver
British Columbia
Canada V5V 3X4

JOAN RIVERS
C/O Bil Sammeth Organisation
9200 Sunset Blvd.
Suite 1001
Los Angeles
California 90069
U.S.A.

May 17 1987

Dear Joan,

    I am scarcely able to comprehend the shocking news in the Entertainment section of my newspaper! Fox Broadcasting Co. claim that your ratings have declined so sharply since you defecated from the <u>Tonight Show</u> with Johnny Carson, that they are obliged to present you with marching orders!

    It would appear they further state that the number of viewers of <u>The Late Show</u> has fallen far below expectation, which I find impossible to believe.

    I recently witnessed the show which hosted accomplished wit and raconteur, Peter Ustinov, who was visibly aghast, as any anticipation of your riveting articulation and breathtaking intellect was quickly dispelled!

    Mercifully, we were spared the bulk of this alarming example of deteriorating broadcasting standards, as it was rendered almost inaudible by the continual and vulgar cacophony from the partisan audience!

    In view of these sobering circumstances, I fail to see how anyone could claim that viewer ratings are below expectation, when it would be a reasonable expectation that absolutely no-one would be watching!

    As a gesture of great malevolence, could you possibly send me a signed photo, Joan? I'd really treasure it, and I enclose five dollars to facilitate same.

    Many thanks, and good luck!

Yours in sympathy,

Bruce West

309-941 West 13th Avenue
Vancouver
British Columbia
V5Z 1P4

Harlequin Enterprises Ltd
225 Duncan Mill Road
Don Mills
Ontario
M3B 1Z3

May 15th 1985

For the attention of Brian Hickey
President North America

Dear Brian,

I am presently completing my latest work, a book of unusual consequence which is a unique diversification from the type of narrative to which my reputation is usually attributed.

I am convinced that the content of this collection will appeal to the taste of the reader for whom your good House caters, and thus offer you first option to publish, subject to my usual terms and stipulations.

Briefly, the book encompasses a tantalising variety of plot, including amongst others the gripping subjects of assassination, foreign travel, drugs, pop stars, Royalty, top level litigation, police corruption, bizarre religious cults, The Armed Forces, The Mounties, prostitution, mail robbery, celebrity banquets, show business, poisoning, multi-million dollar bank deals, company takeovers, murder abroad, corporal punishment, political corruption, imminent World War, women's issues, senior governmental incompetence, high finance, religion, sex, torture and parliamentary scandal!

I know you will be eager to confirm your interest in securing the publishing rights without delay, and look forward to receiving a substantial advance and your proposals by return post.

I enclose two dollars to cover your expenses in this matter.

Yours sincerely,

Bruce West

Enc.

RICHARD H. CHENOWETH
DIRECTOR
VENTURES GROUP

Harlequin Books

225 Duncan Mill Road, Don Mills, Ontario, Canada M3B 3K9
(416) 445-5860   Telex 06-966697

June 12, 1985

Mr. Bruce West
309 - 941 West 13th Avenue
Vancouver, B.C.
V5Z 1P4

Dear Mr. West:

Brian Hickey has asked me to respond to your letter of May 15, 1985
regarding your latest work.

Several aspects of your proposal create problems for me:

. I personally am not familiar with... "The type of narrative
  to which your reputation is usually attributed."

. Again, I am not familiar with your "usual terms and stipulations"
  under which you grant publishing rights.

. Your description of the work is too generalized and inadequate
  to evaluate the work. In an instance such as this, we only
  would consider negotiating for publishing rights upon our
  review of the completed manuscript.

As a result of these problems, I <u>cannot</u> confirm our interest in your work
and will not be forwarding a "substantial advance" or a proposal. I do
enclose your uncashed cheque for $2.00 submitted by you to cover our
expenses in this matter.

Yours truly,

R.H. Chenoweth
Director Ventures Group

RHC:zw

Encl.

309-941 West 13th Avenue
Vancouver
British Columbia
V5Z 1P4

Canada Post Corporation
Confederation Heights
Ottawa
Ontario
K1A 0B1

October 22nd 1984

For the attention of Michael Warren
<u>President</u>

Dear Mr. Warren,

You can imagine my surprise this morning, when I
switched on the radio to hear the news of a possible strike
by postal workers.

Those of us in the business community were completely
unaware that your Corporation was not already on strike!

If the radio report is accurate and your employees
have not yet ceased to function and they do strike, what
possible reduction in postal service could be the result?

A quick survey of my executives indicates conclusively
that the only avenue left open to further deteriorate productivity
would be for you to despatch armed operatives to take back the
mail already delivered!

This course of action would not cause too much
inconvenience to us incidentally, as by the time the mail
arrives it is usually too old to be of value anyway.

I am posting this letter at precisely midday today,
and await with interest the date I receive your reply, which
will serve as a visible measurement of the efficiency of the
postal operation.

Yours sincerely,

Bruce West

Canada Post
Corporation

Société canadienne
des postes

Office of the
President and Chief
Executive Officer

Cabinet du
Président –
directeur général

Ottawa, Canada
K1A 0B1

November 5, 1984

Mr. Bruce West
309 - 941 West 13th Avenue
VANCOUVER, B.C.
V5Z 1P4

Dear Mr. West:

   I am writing to acknowledge receipt of your letter of October 22
to Mr. R. Michael Warren, President of the Canada Post Corporation,
commenting on the postal service.

   Please be assured that your comments have been brought to
Mr. Warren's attention.

                            Yours sincerely,

                            Esther Christopher
                            Manager
                            Correspondence Unit

Canada

309-941 West 13th Avenue
Vancouver
British Columbia
V5Z 1P4

Canada Post Corporation
Ottawa
Ontario
K1A 0B1

November 8th 1984

For the attention of Michael Warren
<u>President</u>

Dear Warren,

     Please thank your assistant, Esther Christopher for
the reply to my letter of October 22nd, which I received this
morning.

     Why can't you answer your own correspondence?

     I went to the trouble of writing to you personally,
why should I not be afforded the reciprocal courtesy?

     If I have occasion to communicate with you again,
I shall address you through my chauffeur.

Yours sincerely,

Bruce West

309-941 West 13th Avenue
Vancouver
British Columbia
V5Z 1P4

The Toronto Stock Exchange
2 First Canadian Place
Toronto
Ontario
M5X 1J2

November 23rd 1984

For the attention of J. Pearce Bunting
<u>President</u>

Dear Mr. Bunting,

     In light of a couple of close shaves with the Constabulary
in recent months, I am obliged to retire from my usual 'business'
for a while, and dispose of the proceeds before we are forcibly
separated!

     I am reliably informed that the Stock Market is not a
bad number to get into if you know your way around, and I gather
one can rely on absolute discretion regarding the origin of the
funds your people accept for investment?

     I have a considerable amount (in cash!) to lay out as
quickly as possible, and as soon as you let me know the score,
I will hot-foot to your Office with the necessary in hand.

     Needless to say, if you can get me pointed in the right
direction with no unnecessary fuss, there will be 'something in it'
for you personally.

     I look forward to your early advice.

Yours sincerely,

Bruce West

The Exchange

The Exchange Tower
2 First Canadian Place
Toronto, Canada M5X 1J2
(416) 947-4700

December 18, 1984

Mr. Bruce West
309-941 West 13th Avenue
Vancouver, B.C.
V5Z 1P4

Dear Mr. West:

Further to your recent letter with regard to investing on the stock
market, I have enclosed some general information which you may find
useful.

The TSE does not buy or sell stocks on behalf of investors. This means
that all business must be transacted through a brokerage firm which is
a member of the TSE. In addition you must select a stockbroker from
the member firm who will act on your behalf. You will be required to
open an account with the brokerage firm before you are permitted to
trade. Your stockbroker will advise you on your investment alternatives.

Should you have any further questions, please don't hesitate to contact
me.

Yours truly,

Mary M. Revell.

Mary M. Revell
Manager,
Information & Media Services

MMR/jc

encls.

309-941 West 13th Avenue
Vancouver
British Columbia
V5Z 1P4

Public Service Commission
P.O. Box 2703
Whitehorse
Yukon Y1A 2C6

December 4th 1984

Dear Sir,

Regarding the advertised vacancy for Territorial Court Judge, you need search no further!

My vast legal expertise has been acquired over a considerable number of years, and to the eternal frustration of my opponents thus far I have a spotless record. How many of us can boast that nowadays?

You may be assured that all who appear before me for sentencing will be well advised to prepare themselves for a long detention, with minimal facilities to ease the passage of time. Yes Sir, I intend to crack down on trouble makers, and crack down hard!

I note the salary for this position is a nominal $74,345.00 per annum. I would also have to insist on an aircraft for my personal transportation, and of course a Motor-Carriage commensurate with the status of the appointment.

I am not without means, and I am on first name terms with the Prime Minister.

I look forward to receiving confirmation of my appointment, and to expedite same I enclose five dollars to make sure my name goes straight to the top of the pile.

Yours faithfully,

Bruce West

Enc.

Yukon

Public Service Commission

Box 2703, Whitehorse, Yukon Y1A 2C6
(403) 667-5811 Telex 036-8-260

Our File:
Your File:

1984 December 11

Mr. Bruce West,
309-941 West 13th Avenue,
Vancouver, B.C.
V5Z 1P4

Dear Mr. West:

I am in receipt of your letter of application dated December 04, 1984
for the position of Territorial Court Judge.

Please be advised that "an aircraft for (my) personal transportation"
and "a motor carriage" are not provided with this position.

I am returning your cheque for five dollars ... any attempt to bribe
a public official is an offence under the Criminal Code.

Yours sincerely,

Susan L. Priest,
Personnel Officer.

/jp

encl.

309-941 West 13th Avenue
Vancouver
British Columbia
Canada V5Z 1P4

Females for Felons
51 E. 42nd Street # 517
New York
N.Y. 10017
U.S.A.

December 17th 1984

For the attention of Ralph Sturges
Co-Ordinator

Dear Ralph,

I am distressed to report that I am about to begin
a stiff jail sentence over the trivial offence of bribing
a Government Official, and I should therefore be grateful
if you could enrol me in your very sensible 'Females for
Felons' scheme without delay, which may take some of the
sting out of this cruel punishment!

What's the procedure? Have you a catalogue? Is
there a fee? Do I send details of my 'preferences'? How
often could one expect a 'visit'?

I look forward to your urgent reply, and for your
convenience enclose a self addressed envelope together with
a dollar to cover postage.

Many thanks.

Yours in adversity,

Bruce West

Enc.

C/O 309-941 West 13th Avenue
Vancouver
British Columbia
Canada V5Z 1P4

Females for Felons
51 E. 42nd Street # 517
New York
N.Y. 10017
U.S.A.

March 19th 1985

For the attention of Ralph Sturges
<u>Co-Ordinator</u>

Dear Ralph,

    For Pity's sake man, what's the hold up?

    I requested details of your service over three
months ago, even going so far as to enclose a dollar to
cover the postage, and thus far you have completely
overlooked my plight!

    Is this any way to treat a fellow Christian
who has fallen by the wayside?

    I await your kind consideration with eager
anticipation and grateful thanks.

                Yours sincerely,

                Bruce West

309-941 West 13th Avenue
Vancouver
British Columbia
Canada V5Z 1P4

Prime Minister Margaret Thatcher
10 Downing Street
London
S.W.1.
<u>GREAT BRITAIN</u>

July 12th 1985

Dear Prime Minister,

As a loyal British subject, I am writing to express the horror and disgust I felt upon reading a most irreverent report in today's newspaper.

If the article is to be believed, the new British One Pound Coin is now officially referred to as a 'Maggie', on the premise that its' unpopularity is based on it comprising a "Cheap brass bit that thinks it's a Sovereign!"

Apart from my personal condemnation of such cruel numismatic treason, I am also concerned that should Canada also adopt a One Dollar Coin to replace the current paper version, Prime Minister Brian Mulroney might well suffer the same disgraceful allegory to the new currency that you are now enduring.

As you know, Mr. Mulroney is a highly sensitive fellow, by no means a man of the world like yourself, and I know that any below the belt reference to his personal image would wound him terribly.

One anticipates with dread the reaction of the visiting Foreigner proffering a new One Dollar Coin, upon being informed that it was now called a 'Brian', because it was "New to the job, swiftly wore a hole in the pocket, and was thoroughly unconvincing to those unfamiliar with it!"

Any counter-measures you may be able to suggest to shore up Mr. Mulroney's reputation should the new coin be introduced here will be most gratefully received.

With many thanks and warm condolances.

Yours sincerely,

Bruce West

Mr B West
309-941 West 13th Avenue
Vancouver
British Columbia
CANADA
V5Z 1P4

Treasury Chambers
Parliament Street
LONDON
SW1P 3AG
Telex 262405
Telephone Direct Line 01-233
Switchboard 01-233 3000

Our reference
12/7/1
28 August 198

Dear Mr West

£1 COIN

You wrote to the Prime Minister on 12 July concerning an article in a newspaper about the £1 coin. I have been asked to reply and should begin by apologising for the delay in doing so.

As I have not seen the newspaper article to which you refer I cannot, of course, comment. But what I can say is that as far as I am aware, the £1 coin does not have an 'official' title, especially that to which you refer in your letter, over and above being referred to by what it is, namely, a £1 coin. That said, the logic that Prime Minister Brian Mulroney might experience a similar fate is not tenable.

Finally, I return the 2 dollar cheque enclosed with your letter.

Yours sincerely

George Haydon.

G C HAYDON

ENC

PG

309-941 West 13th Avenue
Vancouver
British Columbia
Canada V5Z 1P4

The Coca-Cola Company
310 North Avenue N.W.
Atlanta
Georgia 30313   October 2nd 1984
U.S.A.

For the attention of Roberto C. Goizueta
Chairman

Dear Mr. Goizueta,

        In accord with the majority of responsible physicians
in North America, my colleagues and I are extremely concerned
regarding the alleged toxic properties contained by your dubious
products.

        You will no doubt be aware of the soon to be published
Government Report on 'soft drinks', with particular reference to
the alarmingly coincident deterioration of digestive function now
recognised to be a direct consequence of regular consumption of
beverages of your ilk.

        My own people have been conducting a private research
into the harmful effects suffered by innumerable children and young
adults, drawn to innocent addiction by glamorous advertisements
such as the example currently showing on television, featuring the
quintessentially popular song-and-dance mannequin, Jesse Jackson.

        I submit sir, that the irresponsible employment of pop
stars to foist your wares upon the young and impressionable is a
moral and commercial travesty of monumental proportion.

        Aside from one's professional commitment to this
investigation into the detrimental content of your products, which
have always been widely reputed to have corrosive properties, one's
personal view to this end is compounded by the recent inexplicable
disappearance of a caged hamster belonging to a neighbour's
children, subsequent to their playfully 'rewarding' the unfortunate
rodent with a saucer of Coke.

        You may be assured that my staff will be collaborating
our evidence with the findings of the Authorities, and that our
consequent public disclosures will ensure swift curtailment of
your blatant commercial excesses.

                                    Yours sincerely,

                                    Bruce West

A Division of The Coca-Cola Company

P.O. Drawer 1734, Atlanta, Georgia 30301   404 676-2603

October 24, 1984

Consumer Information Center

Mr. Bruce West
309-941 West 13th Avenue
Vancouver
British Columbia
CANADA V5Z 1P4

Dear Mr. West:

Our Chairman of the Board, Mr. Roberto C. Goizueta, has asked me to personally thank you for your letter. We are glad to have this opportunity to respond.

Coca-Cola and all our other soft drinks are wholesome beverages manufactured in compliance with the Federal Food Laws, the laws of all the states and the laws of more than 155 countries throughout the world where the product is marketed. The long history of use of soft drinks without adverse health effects further demonstrates the safety of our products.

We make no nutritional claims for Coca-Cola or our other carbonated soft drinks. In our view, every item in a person's diet need not be nutritional in the sense that it is "good for you" nutritionally. All of our soft drinks are marketed as beverages to be consumed for pleasure and enjoyment. We believe there has always been, and always will be, plenty of room in a balanced diet for consumption of pleasant soft drinks.

In response to your reference to our commercials using Jesse Jackson, I assume you are referring to the commercials of PepsiCo. with singer Michael Jackson. We are not affiliated with these advertisments in any way.

As you may know, the aim of our advertisements through the years has been to depict our products as being refreshing beverages enjoyed with good times, and to portray how they enhance any given situation.

Please know, Mr. West, that The Coca-Cola Company engages in a continuing program of research and development in cooperation with our advertising agencies. Different types of ads are considered in terms of consumer acceptance and all the factors that affect the purchasing decision of consumers. As this program continues, it is helpful to have the benefit of opinions such as yours.

Thank you, again, for taking the time to contact us.

Sincerely,

Patricia Martin
Consumer Information Coordinator

PM/sj

R.J. Reynolds Tobacco Co.
Winston-Salem
North Carolina
27102
U.S.A.

CAMPAIGN to BAN NON-SMOKERS
from PUBLIC PLACES
4625 John Street
Vancouver
British Columbia
Canada V5V 3X4

May 20 1987

For the attention of Gerald H. Long
<u>President</u>

Dear Mr. Long,

My ears were heavily assaulted this morning, by an uninformed oaf ranting through my Wireless Set about the dangers associated with tobacco smoke inhalation, both first-hand and second-hand, which has prompted me to solicit your professional opinion as to why these eccentrics are allowed to foist their bigoted views on the gullible public?

My organisation, C.B.N-S.P.P., is of the opinion that cigarette smoking has never conclusively been proved to be a main cause of respiratory disease and related pestilence, and even if tobacco is a lethal carcinogenic, so what? My grandfather smoked seven packs a day, man and boy, and lived to be over 120, which you must agree is conclusive evidence that smoking <u>prolongs</u> life!

Could you, Sir, as an unbiased expert on tobacco, and the huge profits to be made from flogging the stuff, favor my organisation with a few pertinent facts outlining the benefits of smoking, in order to further our campaign to establish our rights across the Free World?

I look forward eagerly to your sensible views on this important subject!

We would, incidentally, be eternally in your debt if you could find the time to make a speech at our next public rally, which is to be held on July 26, at a venue which will be finalised very shortly.

Yours sincerely,

Bruce West
President
C.B.N-S.P.P.

CAMPAIGN to BAN NON-SMOKERS
from PUBLIC PLACES
104-1037 West Broadway
Vancouver
British Columbia
Canada V6H 1E3

R.J. Reynolds Tobacco Co.
Winston-Salem
North Carolina
27102
U.S.A.

For the attention of Edward A. Horrigan Jr.
<u>Chairman</u>

Dear Mr. Horrigan,

     I went to the not inconsiderable trouble of writing to
your President, Gerald H. Long, on May 20, inviting him to
further the cause of promoting tobacco as a health restorative,
through the Offices of the C.B.N-S.P.P., and to date he has
neglected to afford me the courtesy of an acknowledgement!

     Will you look into this disgraceful dereliction of duty
for me at once, Edward?

     With the medical merchants of doom falling over one
another to turn your valuable crop lands into parking-lots
at the wave of a scalpel, one had assumed my generous offer
would have precipitated an immediate and grateful response.

     Please let me have your urgent explanation!

Yours sincerely,

Bruce West
President
C.B.N-S.P.P.

R.J.Reynolds Tobacco Company
Winston-Salem, N.C. 27102
(919) 777-5000

Miriam G. Adams
Manager, Public Relations Consumer Correspondence
(919) 777-7240

July 15, 1987

Mr. Bruce West
104-1037 West Broadway
Vancouver, British Columbia
CANADA   V6H 1E3

Dear Mr. West:

Thank you for your recent letters, addressed to our executives, and to
which they have asked me to respond on their behalf.

We apologize for not having responded to your earlier letter, in which an
invitation was extended to Mr. Gerald H. Long to speak at the July 26 rally.
We regret there was a breakdown in communication, and it was assumed that
someone had responded and we can only offer our sincere apologies.

We regret that Mr. Long will be unable to speak at the rally as he has
another obligation the same date. Also, we have been approached by other
organizations for speakers on the smoking issue, but we have had to decline
all of these due to lack of staff in providing this service.

With the numerous attacks being made on smoking, it is indeed refreshing
to receive a letter such as yours and to be reassured that not everyone
has accepted without question the adverse publicity the tobacco industry
has received. In this regard, I am enclosing several publications which
may be of interest.

The tobacco industry is also concerned about the charges being made that
smoking is responsible for so many serious diseases. Long before the
present criticism began, the tobacco industry, in a sincere attempt to
determine what harmful effects, if any, smoking might have on human
health, established The Council for Tobacco Research--USA. The industry
has also supported research grants directed by the American Medical
Association. Over the years the tobacco industry has given nearly $130
million to independent research on smoking and health--more than all the
voluntary health associations combined.

Despite all the research which has been done, no ingredient or group of
ingredients, as found in tobacco smoke, has been proven to cause disease
in humans. The answers to the many unanswered smoking and health questions - and the fundamental causes of the diseases often statistically
associated with smoking - we believe can only be determined through much
more scientific research. Our company intends, therefore, to continue to
support such research in a continuing search for answers.

We would like to urge you and your friends to voice your opinion to
Legislators and others who count. Only when enough people begin to speak
up that it is unfair discrimination, will it discontinue.

For further information, you may wish to contact Ms. Jada Smith who is with
The Tobacco Institute, Inc., 1875 I Street, N.W., Suite 800, Washington,
DC 20006, telephone number 1/800-424-9876. Please be sure to mention that
you were referred by R.J. Reynolds Tobacco USA.

We are returning enclosed your check for $2.00 as there is no expense for
the material. It is our pleasure to be of assistance and we hope the
publications will be helpful.

Your support of our company and the tobacco industry is very much appreciated.

Sincerely,

MGA:sdh

Enclosures

309-941 West 13th Avenue
Vancouver
British Columbia
V5Z 1P4

Royal Bank of Canada
1 Place Ville Marie
P.O.Box 6001
Montreal
Quebec H3C 3A9

October 12th 1984

For the attention of Rowland C. Frazee
<u>Chairman</u>

Dear Mr. Frazee,

I made my pile the hard way in the construction caper, through the now obsolete virtues of charging high prices, paying low wages, and refusing to recognise the Unions, and I am now expanding my interests.

To this end I wish to acquire the controlling interest in a major food processing corporation, the identity of which need not concern you as yet, and consequently seek a bank of substance to skilfully lead the project.

Initially I considered engaging the services of American Express, through my acquaintance with James Robinson and Sanford Weill (do you know them?) but I suspect that a venture of this type is outside their preferred field of endeavour, to your advantage if you are able to convince me as to your satisfactory experience in this area.

I am obliged to write to you directly, as the banks out here are staffed entirely by dizzy young girls (even the managers!) and I wouldn't want to confuse their pretty heads with important business matters.

We're talking big money here, and I don't want to risk a cock-up!

If you feel competent to handle this undertaking with despatch, perhaps you might forward your proposals for my personal attention, which I will submit to my Board for full consideration.

Yours sincerely,

Bruce West

THE ROYAL BANK OF CANADA

HEAD OFFICE - BOX 6001
MONTREAL, P.Q. H3C 3A9

D. H. REINHARDT
ASSISTANT TO THE CHAIRMAN
AND CHIEF EXECUTIVE OFFICER

October 18, 1984

Mr. Bruce West
309-941 West 13th Avenue
Vancouver, B.C.
V5Z 1P4

Dear Mr. West:

In Mr. Frazee's absence on a business trip, I
wish to acknowledge receipt of your letter dated
October 12, 1984.

I have forwarded your letter to Mr. L.G. Edmonds,
Vice President of our British Columbia Head-
quarters, in order that he is aware of your
comments.

Yours truly,

THE ROYAL BANK OF CANADA

October 29, 1984

Mr. Bruce West
309-941 West 13th Avenue
Vancouver, B.C.
V5Z 1P4

Dear Mr. West:

Your letter of October 12, 1984, addressed to our Chairman,
Mr. Frazee, has been forwarded to the Independent Business Group
for our attention.

The Royal Bank is the largest lender to business in this Province
and capable of effectively assessing any financial proposition
including your proposed acquisition of a food processing company.
We would welcome an opportunity to discuss this venture with you,
particularly as you are a client of the bank. As we were unable
to contact you by phone today, posibly you could give the writer
a call at 665-4025.

Yours truly,

B.F. Hann
Manager
Independent Business

309-941 West 13th Avenue
Vancouver
British Columbia
V5Z 1P4

Royal Bank of Canada
Box 6001
Montreal
Quebec H3C 3A9

October 31st 1984

For the attention of D. H. Reinhardt

Dear Mr. Reinhardt,

What are you people up to?

Your reply to my enquiry dated October 12th addressed
to your Chairman, informs me that he is away on a 'business'
trip, and that my letter has been forwarded to a Mr. L. G.
Edmonds, who is quite unknown to me, but is apparently
conveniently located approximately 3,000 miles from the
object of my interest!

For whatever reason alas I do not hear from Mr. Edmonds,
but instead from yet another new name, a B. F. Hann who has
discovered my private telephone number and has been calling me
with evident disregard for the confidential aspect of my enquiry.

In light of this extraordinary lack of propriety in
dealing with sensitive financial matters therefore, I have
secured more discreet usurers for my purposes.

Yours sincerely,

Bruce West

Copy to B. F. Hann

309-941 West 13th Avenue
Vancouver
British Columbia
Canada V5Z 1P4

Phil Donahue
The Donahue Show
2501 Bradley Place
Chicago   October 11th 1984
Illinois 60618
U.S.A.

Dear Mr. Donahue,

        I'll come straight to the point. I am putting on a
television show here for a major sponsor, and I want you to
compere it.

        I've been studying your own programme over a number
of weeks, and frankly I'm impressed!

        You have created the perfect formula, three or four
atribilious lesbians ranting over trivial 'womens issues', and
a garrulous audience comprising bored housewives plagued by
gender identity crisis. It works every time and the mugs love
it!

        Here's the plan. The show will be recorded in early
January '85, and my people will organise everything except the
Amazonians and the subject for 'discussion', which I shall leave
up to you.

        I can guarantee a packed paying audience, who will jump
at the chance of a morning's respite from the supermarkets and
their 'exercise' classes.

        What would be your fee Phil, and are you O.K. for
January?

        As soon as I hear from you, my lawyers will submit full
proposals to your advisers, and we can start to make money!

        I look forward to your early confirmation.

        Kindest regards.

                            Yours sincerely,

                            Bruce West

309-941 West 13th Avenue
Vancouver
British Columbia
Canada V5Z 1P4

Phil Donahue
The Donahue Show
2501 Bradley Place
Chicago
Illinois 60618
U.S.A.

December 17th 1984

Dear Phil,

I'm amazed not to have heard from you regarding the
generous offer contained in my letter of October 11th.

Not still thinking it over, surely?

If you are not up to hosting our show, perhaps you
might have the courtesy to let me know. There is no shortage
of people in your line of work we can call upon for the job,
but we must hear from you one way or the other.

I enclose a dollar to cover the cost of postage, in
case things are a bit tight at present.

Yours sincerely,

Bruce West

Enc.

309-941 West 13th Avenue
Vancouver
British Columbia
Canada V5Z 1P4

Phil Donahue
The Donahue Show
2501 Bradley Place
Chicago
Illinois 60618
U.S.A.

February 15th 1985

Dear Phil,

     Good Lord man, what's the hold up?

     We are ready to go here, and you are still
dithering over my offer of October 11th last, and further
reminder and down-payment of December 17th!

     I enclose a further two dollars to help swing
the balance - let's go!

Yours sincerely,

Bruce West

Enc.

Note: No reply received. —Ed.

309-941 West 13th Avenue
Vancouver
British Columbia
Canada V5Z 1P4

President Ronald Reagan
The White House
Washington D.C.
20500   November 9th 1984
U.S.A.

Dear Mr. President,

        So! Another four long years in Office!

        One hopes the predictions that your advanced years
might prevent your completing the full term will not come
to fruition.

        Your critics should not underestimate the presbyopic
capability which so overwhelmingly engineered your successful
continuation in Office.

        Having invested such generous quantities of energy,
guile and money hoodwinking the American voter into believing
that your proclaimed dedication to peace was likely to be
realised after the Polling Booths closed, it would be a blow
indeed if your untimely expiry was to preclude the opportunity
to disprove the popular conjecture that you will now initiate
a proliferation of invasions throughout the world.

        To expedite your reply to this and my letters of
September 6th and October 10th, I enclose a cheque for $1.00
to cover the price of a stamp, on the assumption that even an
American President would not pocket a fellow's postage money!

                                Yours sincerely,

                                Bruce West

Enc.

THE WHITE HOUSE
WASHINGTON

November 21, 1984

Dear Mr. West:

Because the White House is prohibited from accepting monetary gifts or political contributions, we are returning your enclosure. However, the interest which prompted you to write is appreciated.

Sincerely,

Anne Higgins

Anne Higgins
Special Assistant to the President
and Director of Correspondence

Mr. Bruce West
309-941 West 13th Avenue
Vancouver, B.C.
Canada V5Z 1P4

Enclosure: Monetary item returned

309-941 West 13th Avenue
Vancouver
British Columbia
Canada V5Z 1P4

Central Intelligence Agency
Washington
D.C. 20505
U.S.A.

November 26th 1984

For the attention of William J. Casey
<u>Director</u>

Dear Mr. Casey,

I am compelled to bring to your attention a matter of
extreme urgency which demands your immediate investigation.

I have sent despatches to President Ronald Reagan on
three separate occasions, commending the stand of your Great
Country against our mutual adversary the Communist, even going
so far as to donate a substantial sum of money to the cause
with my last communication, and to date I have heard nothing!

Sir, as an expert on National Security, does this not
strike you as very odd?

I have no wish to interfere with the internal affairs
of your Nation, but you must agree that such strange behaviour
indicates that something is seriously amiss in the White House.

In the interest of security, no doubt you will initiate
a thorough enquiry into the background and current activities
of the President, in order to flush out any proclivity toward
unconstitutional political leaning which may have previously
slipped through the CIA net.

I await your full report in early course, and I will be
standing by in case I can assist with my evidence.

Yours sincerely,

Bruce West

309-941 West 13th Avenue
Vancouver
British Columbia
Canada V5Z 1P4

Federal Bureau of Investigation
Department of Justice
Constitution Avenue & Tenth St. N.W.
Washington D.C.
20530
U.S.A.

January 5th 1985

For the attention of William H. Webster
<u>Director</u>

Dear Mr. Webster,

     As a consequence of my involvement with top-level international politics, during a recent exchange of correspondence with President Reagan I uncovered what was in my professional opinion, a Communist infiltration in the White House!

     With no concern for my own personal safety and reputation, I laid my life on the line and revealed my findings in strictest confidence to William J. Casey at the CIA.

     This was over six weeks ago, and the continuing ominous silence from Casey, together with subsequent strange noises from my personal telephone, leads me to suspect to my horror that the rot may be more widespread than I at first suspected!

     On the understanding that the FBI is above suspicion in matters relating to the Eastern Bloc, may I entrust you with the task of a thorough screening of the Casey fellow, to discover if he comes up squeaky-clean in the Marxist department?

     Needless to say, I shall delay exposing all to the Press until I have the go-ahead from you. Mum's the word!

     I enclose a dollar for the convenience of your postage, and await your further instructions.

Yours for a Communist-Free
North America,

Bruce West

Enc.

Washington, D.C. 20535

February 14, 1985

Mr. Bruce West
309-941 West 13th Avenue
Vancouver, British Columbia, Canada
V5Z 1P4

Dear Mr. West:

Your January 5th communication to Judge Webster
has been referred to me for reply. I appreciate your concern.

From the limited data you provided, there is no
indication that a violation of Federal law within the investi-
gative jurisdiction of the FBI has occurred. If you have
additional, more specific information which you believe would
substantiate a violation within our jurisdiction, please
do not hesitate to contact us. I can assure you that any
information you furnish will be given prompt consideration.

I am returning the check you so thoughtfully sent.

Sincerely,

William M. Baker
Assistant Director
Office of Congressional
   and Public Affairs

Enclosure

309-941 West 13th Avenue
Vancouver
British Columbia
Canada V5Z 1P4

Central Intelligence Agency
Washington
D.C. 20505
U.S.A.

February 8th 1985

For the attention of William J. Casey
<u>Director</u>

<u>TOP SECRET</u>

Dear Casey,

Evidently the alarming implications revealed in my
letter of November 26th have not sunk in, as you have yet
to summon me as a prime witness to your investigation of
the White House!

More than likely you are still working under cover,
and I will be called to give evidence any day now?

I can be on your doorstep at a moment's notice, and
to this end I enclose a dollar to cover the cost of the
postage of my Notice To Appear.

Let's go!

Yours sincerely,

Bruce West

Enc.

Central Intelligence Agency

Washington, D.C. 20505

22 February 1985

Mr. Bruce West
309 - 941 W. 13th Avenue
Vancouver, B.C. V5Z 1P4

Dear Sir:

Enclosed is your check for $1.00 that you recently
sent us in the mail.

Please do not send us any money in the future.

Thaddeus P. Brockman

309-941 West 13th Avenue
Vancouver
British Columbia
Canada V5Z 1P4

Liberace
4993 Wilbur Street
Las Vegas
Nevada 89119
U.S.A.

November 15th 1984

Dear Liberace,

     I very much enjoyed seeing one of your shows on the television a few nights ago, and as I watched your richly scintillating yet tasteful performance, I was reminded of my childhood days, when my strange old maiden aunt with an unusual predilection for rather sudden attire of habiliment like yourself, used to entertain my fourteen brothers and sisters and I on the Family Piano in the Drawing Room.

     You were indeed a most moving reminder of those nostalgic years Liberace. My aunt of course has now thankfully passed away, God bless her, and I wonder if I might beg an autographed photo of you in your stage costume, to remind me of those odd, yet in a way joyful years at the mercy of my beloved old relative.

     Thank you in anticipation, and may you continue to give pleasure to millions for many more years.

Yours sincerely,

Bruce West

309-941 West 13th Avenue
Vancouver
British Columbia
Canada V5Z 1P4

Procter & Gamble Co.
301 E. Sixth Street
Cincinatti
Ohio 45202
U.S.A.

December 6th 1984

For the attention of John G. Smale
<u>President</u>

Dear Mr. Smale,

     I am writing to express my profound satisfaction with
your excellent product, new 'Bounce'.

     We operate a large Kennels here, and since switching
all the dogs' diet to 'Bounce', we have observed a marked
improvement in several directions. In particular the animals
are of a more contented disposition, their coats are healthier,
incidence of fleas and mites have decreased, and breeding and
birth-rate are much improved.

     One small point however. As we use such large quantities
on a daily basis, I wonder if you could let me know where we
might be able to obtain a wholesale discount, as our feed bill is
quite substantial? None of our regular suppliers is prepared to
offer a reduction, but I'm sure a word from your good Offices
will swiftly bring them to heel!

     Thank you in anticipation, and should you wish to send a
team to make a television commercial on our premises, they would
be most welcome at any time.

Yours sincerely,

Bruce West

PROCTER & GAMBLE INC.

Post Office Box 355, Station "A", Toronto, Ontario, Canada M5W 1C5 Telephone 924-4661 Area Code 416 Telex 065-24170

February 26, 1985

Mr. Bruce West
309-941 West 13th Ave.
Vancouver, B.C.
V5Z 1P4

Dear Mr. West:

Your recent letter addressed to Mr. John Smale at Procter & Gamble
in the U.S. has been referred to me for a response.

Since our product Bounce is a laundry fabric softener in sheet form
for use in the dryer, I am somewhat puzzled by your enquiry. Is
there another product in the animal food field called Bounce, or
something similar?

Perhaps you could telephone me collect to clarify this.

Yours sincerely,

Barry J. Pipes
Manager, External Affairs

BJP:db

                                        309-941 West 13th Avenue
                                        Vancouver
Procter & Gamble Inc.   British Columbia
P.O. Box 355   V5Z 1P4
Station 'A'
Toronto
Ontario   March 1st 1985
M5W 1C5

For the attention of Barry J. Pipes
Manager, External Affairs

Dear Pipes,

        Good Lord!

        I am most grateful to you for explaining the
purpose for which 'Bounce' is intended, and you may rest
assured that our animals' diet will be corrected with
immediate effect.

        Thank you again for bringing this unfortunate
error to my attention!

                            Yours sincerely,

                            Bruce West

104-1037 West Broadway
Vancouver
British Columbia
Canada V6H 1E3

Oprah Winfrey
35 East Wacker Drive
Suite 1782
Chicago
Illinois 60601   June 12 1987
U.S.A.

Dear Oprah,

    Just switched off the box (television) after watching
yet another of your great shows - congratulations, I never miss
a single performance!

    Mrs. Tirpitz next door and I both agree that you deserve
a medal, for demonstrating to those who question the freedom of
a democratic society, that it is perfectly possible for anyone
to get to the top in show business, no matter how lacking in
talent they may be!

    But tell me, Oprah, what happens when you go on vacation,
or are unavoidably detained negotiating a revolving-door at the
recording studio, or other mishap? The reason I ask is that having
recently quit the night shift at the abbatoir, I'm presently
'in between jobs' and I wonder if you ever need a stand-in?
I should mention straight away that despite the miraculous advances
of modern medical technology, I cannot envisage being either female
or black in the forseeable future, but I don't necessarily view
this as a problem in today's enlightened society!

    On the positive side, I _am_ blessed with a monotonous
baritone voice, and I'm sure with intensive coaching I could
manage to slouch in a chair, or stand around looking out of my
depth clutching a massive microphone, and read: "We'll be right
back", "You're on the air, hello", and "We are out of time"
cue-cards at the back of the studio.

    Let me know what you think!

    One small observation regarding your own appearance.
I'm sure you'd stimulate a much bigger audience if you dressed
in less comprehensive wearing apparel - what's wrong with turning
out in something a little more revealing, even just showing a bit
more leg perhaps?

    No, on second thoughts, I'm sure you know best, why take
unnecessary risks!

    I'd love an autographed photo, Oprah, if possible, and I
enclose two dollars in hopeful anticipation, with grateful thanks
and very best wishes.

                                   Yours sincerely,
                                   Bruce West

P. O. BOX 909715, CHICAGO, ILLINOIS 60690

Aug 15, 1987

Dear Bruce:

Thanks so much for your kindness and your
comments.

Best wishes,

Oprah Winfrey

309-941 West 13th Avenue
Vancouver
British Columbia
Canada V5Z 1P4

Wm. Wrigley Jr. Co.
410 N. Michigan Avenue
Chicago
Illinois 60611
U.S.A.

December 17th 1984

For the attention of William Wrigley
<u>President</u>

Dear Mr. Wrigley,

Our laboratories have been conducting research in order to identify the cause of a particular type of brain malfunction which is demonstrating a serious increase in North America.

We were fairly accurately able to pin down the clinical symptoms of our research, which include moronic staring through glazed eyes, loss of thought co-ordination, inability to grasp simple commands, extreme lethargy, lack of interest in communicating, complete loss of ambition, and sharply reduced speech participation.

For months we were baffled. All the information fed into our computer proved inconclusive.

Then a breakthrough! It transpired that over 98% of our patients were habitual users of chewing gum.

Astonishing though this at first seemed, we double checked our statistics again and again, and the evidence conclusively demonstrates that regular chewing of gum is isolated as the single cause of the gross malfunction of intellectual capacity.

We will be submitting our Paper to the World Health Organisation in early course, and prior to despatching same, we would appreciate hearing your views on this alarming revelation.

Yours sincerely,

Bruce West

Wm. WRIGLEY Jr. Company
WRIGLEY BUILDING • 410 N. MICHIGAN AVENUE
CHICAGO, ILLINOIS 60611

Telephone: 644-2121
Area Code 312

WHOLESOME • DELICIOUS • SATISFYING

December 28, 1984

Mr. Bruce West
309-941 West 13th Avenue
Vancouver
British Columbia
CANADA V5Z 1P4

Dear Mr. West:

We're sorry and somewhat surprised to learn about your negative
attitude toward chewing gum.

Exercising the mouth and jaw muscles through chewing is a
natural instinct that can be traced back thousands of years,
to antiquity. The ancient Greeks, no slouches where civilization
is concerned, chewed the gum of the mastic tree, and the Aztecs,
whose sophisticated culture in Mexico's Yucatan peninsula
flourished a thousand years, raised the enjoyment of chewing
chicle from the native sapodilla trees to a fine art.

Here in America, the New England colonists began making spruce
gum at home 300 years ago, and gum has been commercially available
for more than a century. So I wouldn't become too concerned
about a world decline in intellectual capacity due to chewing
gum, though we agree with you that some folks do seem to display
a lack of old-fashioned common sense these days.

On the positive side, chewing gum helps relieve nervous tension,
eases monotony, provides a quick and convenient pick-me-up,
and is a handy, low-calorie substitute for cigarettes and
fattening snacks. In fact, chewing gum was considered such a
necessity that it was included in Army K-rations during World
War II as a welcome "taste of home" for U.S., Canadian and
British soldiers fighting in the trenches.

I hope the enclosed summary of facts will give you a fresh
perspective on a quality product we've marketed proudly for 92
years. And please enjoy the complimentary packages of Doublemint
gum we're sending you under separate cover.

With best wishes,

WM. WRIGLEY JR. COMPANY

Barbara Sadek

Barbara Sadek

309-941 West 13th Avenue
Vancouver
British Columbia
V5Z 1P4

Rothmans of Canada Ltd
1500 Don Mills Road
Don Mills
Ontario
M3B 3L1

December 11th 1984

For the attention of C. Landmark
<u>Chairman</u>

Dear Mr. Landmark,

I wish to complain in the strongest possible vein over your current magazine advertising.

I have before me a full page colour advertisement for 'Rothmans SPECIAL MILD', which states in bold copy, "Great taste...and they're mild."

How on earth can a small paper cylinder packed with a carcinogenic leaf, which is placed between the lips and ignited for the express purpose of inhalation, possibly be accurately described as producing anything other than a smell, and an unpleasant, addictive and dangerous one at that?

If you and I were in a small elevator together, and I suddenly dropped my pants, bent forward and farted extensively, would you in all honesty exclaim in delight, "Great taste!"? I think not, and I trust you will take my point that the simile is most appropriate to your grossly misleading advertising.

Anyone who has had the misfortune to smell the breath of the cigarette addict is only too aware that the stench could most accurately be described as being close to dog excrement that has been blended with vomit - perhaps as a 'responsible' company Chairman you will consider using this more accurate statement in your next campaign?

Before I report your Company to the Advertising Standards Authority, I shall wait to consider your defence of my points.

Yours sincerely,

Bruce West

Rothmans of Canada Limited

75 DUFFLAW ROAD · TORONTO, ONTARIO M6A 2W4

January 4, 1985

Mr. Bruce West
309 - 941 West 13th Avenue
Vancouver, B.C.
V5Z 1P4

Dear Mr. West:

We acknowledge receipt of your recent letter concerning the advertising of cigarettes. For your information, Rothmans of Canada Limited is a holding company not directly involved in the manufacture and marketing of tobacco products but in spite of this, we feel compelled to briefly respond to your letter.

Needless to say, we greatly deplore the examples and analogies used in your letter. They reveal a complete ignorance of the reasons why millions of Canadians use this product daily.

However, you are allowed in this free country of ours, to express your opinion and we respect that right. I would hope that you would do the same when it comes to cigarette advertising.

Yours very truly,

C.A. Denis

309-941 West 13th Avenue
Vancouver
British Columbia
V5Z 1P4

'Thrill of a Lifetime'
Box 9
Station 'O'
Toronto
Ontario

December 12th 1984

For the attention of Doug Paulson

Dear Doug,

        I watch your most entertaining television show every
week without fail, and may I say how much pleasure I derive
from it.

        My 'Thrill of a Lifetime' would be to be flown first-
class to Bangkok, and spend a weekend locked in a very small
room with a dozen young ladies covered from head to foot in body
oil, with whom I could reduce myself to an exhausted basket-case
at the end of the 48 hours!

        I should then like to be flown home (first-class of
course) under appropriate medical supervision, with a video
cassette of the vacation highlights to remind myself in my old
age of the generosity of your programme.

        In order to expedite the processing of my Thrill, I
enclose a deposit of five dollars, and look forward to receiving
a list of dates which would be suitable to you for this marathon.

                                        Yours sincerely,

                                        Bruce West

Enc.

309-941 West 13th Avenue
Vancouver
British Columbia
V5Z 1P4

'Thrill of a Lifetime'
Box 9
Station 'O'
Toronto
Ontario

February 13th 1985

<u>For the attention of The Producer</u>

Dear Sir,

     I have been sitting here with my bags packed since December 12th last, when I sent five dollars to Doug Paulson as a deposit for the expedition of my 'Thrill of a Lifetime'.

     How long do these things take?

     Will Mr. Paulson be sending me a receipt for my five dollars soon?

     Please let me have your instructions by return of post.

Yours in anticipation,

Bruce West

Editor's Note: CFTO-TV returned Mr. West's cheque but didn't tell him why.

309-941 West 13th Avenue
Vancouver
British Columbia
Canada V5Z 1P4

Her Majesty Queen Elizabeth ll
Buckingham Palace
London S.W.l.
<u>GREAT BRITAIN</u>

April 16th 1985

Your Majesty,

        Will the Gutter Press never cease their hounding
innocent members of the Royal Family in order to increase
the circulation of their disgraceful Comics?

        The disclosure in today's papers that Princess Michael
of Kent is the daughter of a Nazi S.S. Officer, in my humble
opinion is an unpardonable infringement of the respect and
privacy to which your family should be entitled.

        Good Lord, we all have our share of skeletons in the
cupboard, why I myself have an uncle (twice removed) who is
a practising Socialist!

        Do I allow snooping reporters to blacken my good name
by revealing all in the working-class Media? No Ma'am!

        It is high time the Press was taught to behave with
greater responsibility when covering sensitive issues which
can confuse the less enlightened reader. I am quite sure
that Baron Gunther von Reibnitz was at heart just an ordinary
working family man, who enjoyed a relaxing evening in front
of the T.V. with the wife and kids after a hard days' interrogation
at the Office, just like the rest of us!

        Here's five dollars. Please use it to 'dissuade' Daily
Mirror reporters from overstepping the mark on any future
disclosures of this nature.

                              Your loyal subject,

                              Bruce West

Enc.

BUCKINGHAM PALACE

1st May, 1985

Dear Mr West.

The Queen has commanded me to thank you
for your letter about The Prince and Princess of
Wales' visit to the Vatican. Any decision on
The Prince of Wales' programme is taken by His
Royal Highness. On the content of the
programme, The Prince of Wales receives advice
from many quarters, as was the case on this
particular occasion.

I am returning your cheque for 5 dollars
herewith.

Yours Sincerely
Robert Fellow.

Bruce West, Esq.

BUCKINGHAM PALACE

2nd May, 1985

Dear Mr West.

I must apologise for my letter of
yesterday which, as you will have realised
by now, was sent to you as the result of a
mix-up in the large weight of correspondence
which The Queen has received recently both
on the subject of The Prince and Princess of
Wales' visit to the Vatican and about the
publicity surrounding Princess Michael of
Kent and her family.

Her Majesty was grateful to you for
writing as you did on the latter subject.

Yours Sincerely
Robert Fellow.

Bruce West, Esq.

309-941 West 13th Avenue
Vancouver
British Columbia
Canada V5Z 1P4

Sikorsky Aircraft
N. Main Street
Stratford
Connecticut 06602
U.S.A.

May 15th 1985

For the attention of William F. Paul
<u>President</u>

Dear Mr. Paul,

I am obliged to purchase a new helicopter as soon as possible, as our present model has unfortunately been destroyed through a misunderstanding with some over-zealous foreign vigilantes.

The new machine will be used primarily for the express transportation of 'vegetable substances' in South America, and must therefore be able to accommodate a payload of around 1,000 lbs plus pilot and two other personnel.

Speed and low-level maneuverability are vital considerations, as is availability in camouflage paintwork for mainly night flying over rough terrain. Do you supply fixed armourments (two light machine-guns should be sufficient), and what is the current quoted lead time for delivery? I emphasise again that possession at the earliest is of the utmost priority.

Please send full details and prices by return post, for my personal attention.

I enclose five dollars to cover your expenses, and thank you in anticipation.

Yours sincerely,

Bruce West

Enc.

**UNITED
TECHNOLOGIES
SIKORSKY
AIRCRAFT**

North Main Street
Stratford, Connecticut 06601
(203) 386-4000

June 17, 1985   IML-CAN-WED-85-0308

Mr. Bruce West
309-941 West 13th Avenue
Vancouver
British Columbia
Canada V5Z 1P4

Dear Mr. West:

In response to your letter of May 15, 1985 to Mr. Paul, we are pleased
to provide you with a specification and pictures of our S-76A
helicopter. This is the smallest commercial aircraft that we are
producing at this time. It is a 10,300 pound gross weight machine with
a useful load of 4,700 pounds. A review of the attached data will show
that the S-76 would meet or exceed your requirements. The fly away
price, depending on options and equipment, is approximately $3 million
in U.S. dollars. Delivery is established when the configuration is
determined.

At this time we would like to point out that we do not sell weapons and
that the end use of the machine would have to be determined before a
U.S. export license could be obtained. If this is a government
sanctioned operation, it might be more expeditious to have your customer
procure the helicopter.

Since we do not charge for marketing literature, we are returning your
check for five dollars. Thank you for thinking of Sikorsky to meet your
helicopter needs.

Sincerely,

UNITED TECHNOLOGIES CORPORATION

W. E. Drury/dhw

W. E. Drury, Jr
International Programs
SIKORSKY AIRCRAFT SALES

/dhw

SIKORSKY S-76 MARK II

UTILITY TRANSPORT

Certification:
FAR 29 Amendment 10 as an IFR Transport Category A helicopter.
Proven New Technology:
More performance with less maintenance and lower operating costs.

- **Twin Engines – Flat rated to 1000', 90°F.**
  - Single stage centrifugal compressor – 8.5 to 1 compression ratio.
  - Engine turbine blade containment.

- **Main Rotor Blade**
  - High strength, non-corrosive titanium spar.
  - Non-linear high twist blade – greater lifting performance.
  - Swept trapezoidal tip – more speed with less noise.

- **Articulated Rotor Hub Design – Lower blade and hub stresses**
  - Elastomeric Bearing – eliminates hub lubrication.
  - Bifilar vibration absorber – reduces airframe stresses, maintenance man hours, and increases component life.

- **Tail Rotor Assembly**
  - Cross beam design – 2/3 fewer parts.
  - Composite graphite spar construction.
  - No feathering or flapping bearings to maintain or service.

- **Main Transmission** – simple 3-stage gear reduction system with dual lubricating pumps and redundant accessory drive system.

- **Flight Control System**
  - Fully independent dual hydraulic systems.
  - Dual hydraulic primary servo actuators with automatic by-pass and jam-proof servo valves.
  - Dual SAS/AFCS (optional equipment) components.
  - SAS FAA certification with one system inoperative.

- **Airframe Structure**
  - Multiple load paths, redundant structure.
  - Integral airframe-mounted auxiliary floatation (option).
  - Main Transmission structure designed to 20g forward, 20g downward, and ± 10g sideward loads.

Weights
Maximum Gross Weight	10,300 lb	4,671 kg
Useful Load	4,700 lb	2,131 kg
Standard Fuel Capacity	281 gal	1,064 liters

Performance
Maximum Speed	155 kt	287 km/hr
Maximum Cruise Speed	145 kt	269 km/hr
Best Range Speed	135 kt	250 km/hr
Single Engine Service Ceiling	5,200 ft	1,585 m.
Maximum Range (30 minute reserve)	404 n.m.	748 km.
Fuel Consumption at maximum cruise	610 lb/hr.	277 kg/hr.

Seating Capacity
VFR Configuration	1 pilot
	13 passengers
IFR Configuration	2 pilots
	12 passengers
Executive Configuration	4 to 8 passengers

Dimensions
Main Rotor Diameter (blade tip circle)	44 ft. 0 in.	13.41 m.
Tail Rotor Diameter (blade tip circle)	8 ft. 0 in.	2.44 m.
Wheel Base	16 ft. 5 in.	5.00 m.
Passenger Cabin Length	8 ft. 1 in.	2.46 m.
Passenger Cabin Width	6 ft. 4 in.	1.93 m.
Passenger Cabin Height	4 ft. 5 in.	1.35 m.
Cabin Volume	204 ft.³	5.78 m.³
Baggage Compartment Volume	38 ft.³	1.08 m.³

Engines
Two Detroit Diesel Allison 250-C30S free turbine engines.
Ratings: Per engine, Standard Day, at Sea Level.

2½ Minute Power (OEI), S.L., 90°F	700 shp
Take-off	650 shp

UNITED TECHNOLOGIES
SIKORSKY AIRCRAFT

PAYLOAD/RADIUS

OPTIONAL EQUIPMENT
- Standard S-76 Options
- Planned Utility Options
  - High Clearance, Fixed Gear
  - High Strength Self-sealing Fuel Tank
  - Armored Pilot Seats
  - Troop Seats
  - Cargo Floor
  - Low Pressure Tires

No. of Troops @ 180 lb. (81.6 Kg)

Payload Outbound Only

Best Range Speed

Radius N. Mi.
Radius - Kilometers

GENERAL ARRANGEMENT

Anheuser-Busch Inc
One Busch Plaza
St. Louis
Minnesota 63118
U.S.A.

4625 John Street
Vancouver
British Columbia
Canada V5V 3X4

May 25 1987

For the attention of Dennis P. Long
<u>President</u>

Dear Mr. Long,

I thoroughly enjoyed watching the Indianapolis 500 Motor Race
on the television yesterday, boy, those cars really do shift don't
they! I was particularly inspired by the performance of last year's
winner, Bobby Rahal, in the Lola sponsored by 'Budweiser' beer, which
I understand is brewed by your Company.

As the race progressed, I became increasingly impressed by the
amazing speed at which the pit stops were completed, but I was
particularly startled to see that Rahal's car was being fueled from
a tank filled with 'Budweiser'! I remember not many years back, all
the refueling tanks would bear the legendary names such as Texaco,
Mobil, Amoco and so forth. Such is the progress of modern technology!

I'm not a beer drinker myself, as unlike the imbibers featured in
your advertisements, who seem to be launched into frenzied rapture at
the merest whiff of the stuff, I find that drinking beer causes me to
lapse into unconsciousness and fall over. But having seen all the
advertised claims as to the powers of this magic elixir confirmed live
in Rahal's car, I went out first thing this morning and purchased three
24-packs of 'Budweiser' at a cost of $59.10, and spent over two hours
decanting the 72 bottles into the gas tank of my 1979 Volkswagen
Scirocco, which, by the way, is not as easy as you might suppose!

I was the object of some curious looks from passers by, who were
plainly unaware that I knew something they didn't, but I persevered,
and when the tank was full, I started the engine.

The car started immediately, and I drove off, eagerly anticipating
a substantial increase in power. I had barely selected third gear
however, when the car started to misfire badly, and then stalled.
I tried for some time to re-start it, but to no avail, and in the
process, to make matters worse, caused the battery to go flat.

I am completely baffled, and not a little annoyed! Do Indy
drivers have access to a more potent 'Budweiser' than the man in the
street, or perhaps the canned version is brewed to a higher octane
rating than the bottled?

Please let me have your urgent explanation.

Yours sincerely,

Bruce West

 *Anheuser-Busch, Inc.*
ONE OF THE ANHEUSER-BUSCH COMPANIES

Jack MacDonough
Vice President
Brand Management

June 5, 1987

Mr. Bruce West
4625 John Street
Vancouver
British Columbia
Canada V5V 3X4

Dear Mr. West:

We have received your letter regarding our Indianapolis sponsor-
ship. We are sorry that the broadcast may have misled you into
believing that putting Budweiser in your fuel tank will give you
extra power. Your specific question was "Do Indy drivers have
access to a more potent Budweiser than the man in the street?".
The simple answer is they do not.

On the other hand, if you were a close viewer of the Indianapolis
500 broadcast, you should have noted that regardless of whether
it was Budweiser or another form of alcohol flowing into Bobby
Rahal's car, his car only lasted a short amount of time in the
race. That alone should have warned you not to put Budweiser in
your car. It is perhaps possible that your car, running on
Budweiser, lasted longer than his car running on real fuel.

Incidentally, just so you don't make any mistakes in the future
after watching racing broadcasts, Penzoil only makes lubricating
oil and yet their fuel tank says Penzoil. I recommend you not
put Penzoil in your fuel tank. More importantly, Domino Pizza,
the sponsor on Al Unser, Jr.'s car, and prominantly displayed
on the side of their fuel cans, in no way can power your car.
Although, if ordered with enough pepperoni, it does generate gas.

Sincerely,

Jack MacDonough

Jack MacDonough

JNM:mjk

cc: Dennis P. Long

Executive Offices
One Busch Place
St. Louis, MO U.S.A. 63118-1852
Telex 447 117 ANBUSCH STL

309-941 West 13th Avenue
Vancouver
British Columbia
Canada V5Z 1P4

H. R. H. The Prince of Wales
Buckingham Palace
London S.W.1.
<u>GREAT BRITAIN</u>

December 22nd 1984

Your Royal Highness,

I was deeply disturbed to read in my paper this morning that your sister Princess Anne, in a fit of pique, snubbed the Christening of young Prince Harry in favour of a day's hunting with that frightful husband of hers.

The pretext for this appalling display of manners is ascribed to your not asking Her Highness to be godparent to the young Prince, a decision incidentally which I wholeheartedly endorse!

I don't doubt that in this age of declining standards it is extremely difficult to select godparents of the high calibre necessary to accommodate an heir to the throne, and I am therefore pleased to respectfully submit my name for inclusion on the godparent short-list.

For your interest, I am a loyal British subject of the same generation as yourself, keen on hunting and fishing, have a clean drivers' Licence and no police record, always vote Conservative, and never wear a woolly jumper under a suit. I am also on first name terms with Prime Minister Brian Mulroney (I assume this is a plus!).

I would consider it a great privilege Sir, to receive favourable consideration for this honourable duty.

I shall be in London in the New Year, as I have to discuss my appointment as Secretary-General of the Commonwealth Parliamentary Association with old Sir Robin Vanderfelt, and I look forward to meeting Your Highness then, when we can discuss Prince Harry's future at greater length. May I provisionally suggest lunch on Tuesday January 28th? I look forward immensely to your confirmation that this will be convenient to you.

Yours sincerely,

Bruce West

309-941 West 13th Avenue
Vancouver
British Columbia
Canada V5Z 1P4

H. R. H. The Prince of Wales
Buckingham Palace
London S.W.1.
<u>GREAT BRITAIN</u>

January 21st 1985

Your Royal Highness,

      Further to my letter of December 22nd, I very much
regret that I shall have to postpone our luncheon engagement
for January 28th, as my meeting with Sir Robin Vanderfelt has
been adjourned whilst I conclude the delicate negotiation of
my imminent investiture as President of Mount Saint Vincent
University.

      May I suggest we meet at the latter end of February,
at the convenience of Your Highness?

      I enclose a self-addressed envelope for your expedience
together with a dollar to cover postage, and look forward to
receiving your confirmation of a time suitable for our meeting.

      Kindest regards.

                        Your loyal servant,

                        Bruce West

Encs.

BUCKINGHAM PALACE

From: Equerry to H.R.H. The Prince of Wales

21st February 1985.

Dear Mr West,

    The Prince of Wales has asked me to thank you
for your letter of 21st January.

    His Royal Highness was grateful to you for writing
as you did and asks me to send you his sincere thanks
and best wishes.

Yours sincerely

Peter Eberle

Lieutenant-Commander Peter Eberle, RN.

Mr. Bruce West.

309-941 West 13th Avenue
Vancouver
British Columbia
Canada V5Z 1P4

The Kremlin
Moscow
U.S.S.R.

December 26th 1984

For the attention of Konstantin Chernenko
Chairman of the Presidium of the
Supreme Soviet of the U.S.S.R.

Dear Mr. Chernenko,

Like most western observers, I viewed the invasion of
Afghanistan by the U.S.S.R. some five years ago as a gross and
unwarranted intrusion of the worst possible kind.

Subsequently however, through the educational medium of
television corroboration, my eyes have been opened to the adversity
your hard-pressed forces are having to endure in their efforts to
maintain civil obedience in the hostile terrain of your unwilling
neighbours.

It is all too easy to criticise an army equipped with the
latest weapon technology from a country with a population of over
240 million, as they endure terrible hardships such as home-sickness,
vodka rationing, no television and who knows what other horrors, while
they relentlessly devastate their way through a small country with
a population of under 15 million, some of whom have the audacity to
defend themselves with rudimentary and antiquated small-arms!

Small wonder that tempers are running short in the Kremlin,
as despite the overwhelming odds, the handful of untrained Afghan
tribesmen continually thwart your crack troops, with losses on your
side dumfounding your Generals and causing loss of Military face in
the eyes of your critics.

As a small demonstration of my sympathy for your beleaguered
forces, I enclose two dollars. Buy the lads some woolly socks - I
should not be able to sleep at night for thinking of them catching
colds in those draughty helicopter gun-ships, as they dash about
here and there firing their lethal rockets at pockets of tribesmen
heavily armed with the latest clubs and sharpened sticks with which
to defend themselves and their families from your stabilising
influence.

Yours sincerely,

Bruce West

309-941 West 13th Avenue
Vancouver
British Columbia
Canada V5Z 1P4

The Kremlin
Moscow
U.S.S.R.

February 18th 1985

For the attention of Konstantin Chernenko
Chairman of the Presidium of the
Supreme Soviet of the U.S.S.R.

Dear Mr. Chernenko,

    Is there any foundation to the reassuring rumour of
your recent death, or at least, serious illness which is making
your appearances in public conspicuous by their absence?

    You will understand my natural concern, as I have not
received your reply to my letter and contribution of December 26th
last, and I therefore fear the worst.

    Perhaps you or your next of kin will be good enough to
let me know the current position?

    I enclose a further two dollars to go towards your
medical bills or funeral expenses, whichever is appropriate!

                              Yours sincerely,

                              Bruce West

Enc.

309-941 West 13th Avenue
Vancouver
British Columbia
Canada V5Z 1P4

The Kremlin
Moscow
U.S.S.R.

March 25th 1985

For the attention of Mikhail Gorbachev
Chairman of the Presidium of the
Supreme Soviet of the U.S.S.R.

Dear Mr. Gorbachev,

It is with a profound sense of relief that I find myself able to extend a warm welcome to you as the new leader of the Soviet Union!

One hesitates to speak ill of the dead, but I recently initiated an enlightening exchange of important views with your predecessor Konstantin Chernenko, whereupon the fellow unfortunately passed on, which is frightfully bad form you'll agree? In an effort to further the cause of harmonious East-West relations, I also went to the trouble of including a couple of substantial financial donations to the Cause, which I am saddened to report were not even acknowledged by the Late Leader.

Not that one cares particularly about the money you understand, but as a matter of common courtesy I should appreciate your looking into the matter for me when you have a minute.

You may also be aware that I am a close personal adviser to our Prime Minister, as the enclosed letter from Brian (Mulroney) will demonstrate, and it is my pleasure Sir to assure you that despite what you may have learned to the contrary, he is not a bad type at all!

I look forward to hearing from you with regard to the disappearance of my contributions to The Party through Mr. Chernenko, and enclose a further five dollars to cover your expenses.

Needless to say, if ever yourself and the good Mrs. Gorbachev are visiting these parts, it will be my privilege to entertain the pair of you with a spot of tea on my Lawn!

Yours sincerely,

Note: No reply received. —Ed.

Bruce West

The Kremlin
Moscow
U.S.S.R.

For the attention of Mikhail Gorbachev
Chairman of the Presidium of the
Supreme Soviet of the U.S.S.R.

Dear Comrade Chairman!

Before going to the trouble of starting this missive, I considered
the futility of such a gesture, in view of the fact that I have not yet
received a reply to my last letter to you, dated March 25, 1985!
I realise that lucid communication is not generally recognised to be an
activity for which your Country enjoys international acclaim, but one
has always assumed that even third-world leaders are instructed in the
rudiments of reading and writing?

Anyway, let's not start off on an acrimonious note. My reason for
getting in touch with you again, Mikhail, is to endorse your very sound
and necessary decision to relieve Minister of Defense, Sergei Sokolov,
of his position, following his gross negligence in permitting a teenage
bank clerk to calmly fly through your impenetrable defense network in
broad daylight, and land at the Kremlin steps, in the middle of Red Square!
Fortunately, the ever alert, crack unit of Red Square Police, who are
charged with the task of shielding Central Government from any intruders,
were able to effect a lightning arrest after a couple of hours or so, when
the young pilot gave himself away by allowing authorities to spot him
enjoying a quick snack by his parked 'plane, in between a busy schedule
of interviews and autographing sessions!

The point is, Comrade, that by a quite astounding stroke of good
fortune, I have recently been appointed Sales Distributer of an ingenious
high-technology advanced warning and detection system, which if issued to
every conscript in your dinosaurian armed forces, will prevent the likes
of young Mathias Rust from ever penetrating your defenses again!
These ultra sophisticated protection mechanisms are simple enough for even
Soviet forces to grasp, and although they have yet to be issued with an
official security clearance, they have been effectively tested and proven
in field conditions, under the top-secret code name: "Spectacles", or:
"Eyeglasses"!

In order to demonstrate these cunning little devices to your Generals,
I will be making a sales trip to Moscow next month, in my private 1939
Junkers Ju 87 Stuka Sturzkampfflugzeng, liveried in the family escutcheon
of dayglo yellow and orange stripes. No need to make formal arrangements
for my reception, as I'll probably be flying overnight, and wouldn't want
to disturb anyone before breakfast, but as soon as I've landed and chocked
my wheels, I will tap on your door to let you know I've arrived!

Meanwhile, I enclose two dollars. Please purchase a stout broom, and
have your best man give Red Square a thorough sweeping, as my aircraft is
sensitive to sharp objects, and I should not wish to have my historic sales
visit marred by a punctured landing wheel!

I look forward to meeting you at last!

Yours sincerely,

Bruce West

Enc.

309-941 West 13th Avenue
Vancouver
British Columbia
V5Z 1P4

Air Canada
Place Ville-Marie
Montreal
Quebec
H3B 3P7

December 29th 1984

For the attention of Claude I. Taylor
<u>President</u>

Dear Claude,

        I have been seeking to purchase a suitable airline for
some months, and now that the Government has wisely decided to
get shot of Air Canada, I should be pleased to receive the
Prospectus for Sale together with current Balance Sheet by
return of post.

        Having had the misfortune to be a victim of your
'efficiency' in the past, I am bound to say you are not at the
top of my shopping list, but I am confident that with some
drastic hatchet wielding, my Accountants will soon lick things
into shape.

        All top management and executives will have to be
replaced of course, and complete staff re-training will be a
top priority.

        With diligent pruning and efficient management, I see
no reason why Air Canada should not be able to operate like a
proper airline in very early course.

        As an indication of my serious intention of acquisition,
I enclose a deposit of five dollars, which kindly receipt together
with early despatch of your Prospectus.

                                    Yours sincerely,

                                    Bruce West

Enc.

AIR CANADA ✳ PLACE AIR CANADA, MONTRÉAL, CANADA H2Z 1X5
CABLE-CÂBLE: AIRCANADA   TELEX-TÉLEX: 06-217537

OFFICE OF THE PRESIDENT
BUREAU DU PRÉSIDENT

January 28, 1985

Mr. Bruce West
309-941 West 13th Ave.
Vancouver, B.C.
V5Z 1P4

Dear Mr. West:

This is to acknowledge your letter of December 29th which was
referred to me for reply.

You are no doubt aware that Prime Minister Brian Mulroney
recently announced that Air Canada was not up for sale. We
must, therefore, decline your generous offer and return your
deposit cheque. I realize this will be a disappointment for
you, however, I do hope you will understand our position.

Yours very truly,

N. Duquette

N. Duquette
Supervisor, Customer Relations

Enc.

309-941 West 13th Avenue
Vancouver
British Columbia
Canada V5Z 1P4

The Vatican
Rome
ITALY

December 30th 1984

<u>For the attention of Pope John Paul 11</u>

Your Holiness,

As the morals of the world continue to skate downhill like a greased pig, it is refreshing indeed to listen to your iterative pontifical bringing home to us the inspired words of syllogistic rectitude.

As this planet teeters on the brink of starvation through chronic overpopulation, you sensibly ordain abstention from the use of contraceptives.

As millions of couples endure unbearable lives of relations with their spouses at an end, you persist in refusing to recognise divorce.

Truly your apostolic perspicacity is a blessing and a source of comfort and relief to all men of reason.

There are wicked cynics among us who are of the misguided opinion that an elderly celibate bachelor is not competent to be charged with responsibility for the direction of the lives of over 600 million Catholics. Naturally I do not number myself among such misanthropes. On the contrary, I feel that you should go further still, and ban the disgraceful activities which lead to birth control and divorce, namely copulation and marriage!

I enclose three dollars. Slip into something less ostentatious than your usual attire, and pop downtown incognito one night and enjoy yourself. That should hopefully silence unkind critics of your curious lifestyle once and for all!

Yours sincerely,

Bruce West

Enc.

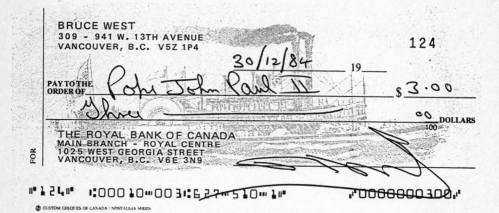

BRUCE WEST
309 - 941 W. 13TH AVENUE
VANCOUVER, B.C. V5Z 1P4

124

30/12/84   19____

PAY TO THE
ORDER OF   Pope John Paul II $ 3.00

Three   00/100 DOLLARS

THE ROYAL BANK OF CANADA
MAIN BRANCH - ROYAL CENTRE
1025 WEST GEORGIA STREET
VANCOUVER, B.C. V6E 3N9

FOR

⑴"124"⑴ ⑴:000 10⑴003:627⑴510⑴1"⑴   ⑴"0000000300"⑴

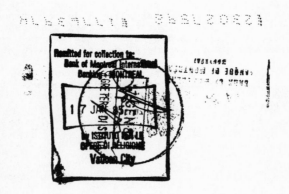

Remitted for collection to:
Bank of Montreal International
Banking - MONTREAL

17 JAN 85

Vatican City

The Vatican
Rome
ITALY

For the attention of Pope John Paul 11

Your Holiness,

        I see from my latest Bank statement/returned cheques
that you did indeed take my advice of the last paragraph in
my letter of December 30th, as my cheque was cashed by you on
January 17th!

        How did you make out?

        As you may imagine, I am a little disappointed that
you saw fit to accept my suggestion and donation without even
so much as a 'thank you', or even found time to comment on the
important theological issues raised in my letter?

        Perhaps you will answer my concerns when your busy
schedule permits, but in the meantime kindly forward a receipt
for my three dollars by return of post.

        Thank you.

                                        Yours sincerely,

                                        Bruce West

309-941 West 13th Avenue
Vancouver
British Columbia
Canada V5Z 1P4

February 10 1985

Commander Matt Koehl
National Socialist White People's Party
2507 N. Franklin Road
Arlington
Virginia 22201
U.S.A.

Commander Koehl:

Since to Canada from my own country I have been
coming, I am missing greatly the rallies with my comrades
we are used to be having.

And so I would like to be your Nazi Party joining
with your permission!

From good Aryan family I am born; also have expert
shooting; in the next uprising am keen to be marching; and
in the head not entirely alright being.

What are your uniforms having? Still mine I am
keeping from the old days!

From you I will be hearing when it is possible
for me to meet for discuss of what is necessary to be done!

Yours truly:

B. von West

309-941 West 13th Avenue
Vancouver
British Columbia
Canada V5Z 1P4

March 25 1985

Commander Matt Koehl
National Socialist White People's Party
2507 N. Franklin Road
Arlington
Virginia 22201
U.S.A.

Commander Koehl:

What for are you to my letter February 10 not
replying?

This is not the efficiency we would be expecting
of the Commandant of a superior peoples!

I am now the urgent reply wanting, and here is
one dollar for the post stamp cost.

Yours truly:

B. von West

Enc. $1

May 1, 1985

B. von West
309-941 W. 13th Ave.
Vancouver, B.C.
Canada V5Z 1P4

Sir;

   We are not knowing what you with your letter of recent date
are meaning.

   We would therefore pleased be if you would to us be explaining.

                              Sincerely,

                              James Ring

                              James Ring

P.O. Box 88
Arlington, VA 22210

Folk Art USA 22

B. von West

309-941 W. 13th Ave.

Vancouver, British Columbia

Canada V5Z 1P4

W.A.N.K.
309-941 West 13th Avenue
Vancouver
British Columbia
Canada V5Z 1P4

Billy Graham Evangalistic Association
1300 Harmon Place
Minneapolis
Minnesota 54403
U.S.A.

October 24th 1984

For the attention of Billy Graham

Your Reverence,

I have long admired your sensible interpretation of
religionist epistemology, and the outstanding inculcation
with which your congregation is induced to contribute to the
expenses of your Church.

In fact you have filled me with such inspiration,
that I have been moved to form a new religious order.

It is called the West Atonement Neighbourhood Kinship
(W.A.N.K. for short, an acronym that rolls crisply off the
tongue you'll agree).

I must emphasise straight away that under no
circumstances will our doctrine tread on the toes of your
fine Order. However, in the early stages of our development,
I would be very appreciative of any advice or assistance you
might be able to impart.

A few old sermon scripts, cassette tapes of some of
your more puissant deliveries, or even just some details of
how to oil the wheels of a productive financial department.

It goes without saying I am more than willing to pay
any charges you deem appropriate for your kind assistance.

Many thanks in anticipation.

Yours sincerely,

Bruce West

P.S.   Could you also oblige with a signed photograph of
       yourself as a personal memento?

1300 Harmon Place, Minneapolis, Minnesota 55403 U.S.A.
101 St. Andrew's House, Sydney Square, N.S.W. 2000, Australia
27 Camden Road, London, NW1 9LN, England
8 Villa du Parc Montsouris, F-75014 Paris, France
P.O. Box 870, Auckland, New Zealand
Incorporated—a non-profit organization

 Billy Graham EVANGELISTIC ASSOCIATION OF CANADA

Room 402—171 Donald Street; mailing address: Box 841, Winnipeg, Manitoba R3C 2R3   (204) 943-0529

November 9, 1984

Mr. Bruce West
W.A.N.K.
309-941 West 13th Avenue
Vancouver BC V5Z 1P4
CANADA

Dear Mr. West:

Thank you for your letter to Mr. Graham mentioning the new religious
order which you plan to form. Mr. Graham is currently away; therefore,
it is my privilege to correspond with you.

Since Mr. Graham will not be back to this office for a number of weeks,
he will not be able to share with you any suggestions he might have
concerning the establishment of your organization. We regret that he
cannot be of help to you at this time. Thank you for writing to him.

Sincerely yours,

Dr. Victor B. Nelson
Executive Assistant

VBN:mh

309-941 West 13th Avenue
Vancouver
British Columbia
Canada V5Z 1P4

Penthouse
909 Third Avenue
New York
N.Y. 10022
U.S.A.

March 22nd 1985

For the attention of Bob Guccione
Editor

Dear Bob,

I have just returned from a highly successful photographic trip to the Bahamas, where I spent two months immortalising a variety of exquisite models for publication in a quality magazine of the Penthouse type.

The girls chosen for my Portfolio were of the highest possible physical calibre, from Asia and Africa as well as European stock, and besides the usual individual shots, I have some rare 'group relationship' poses, together with some singularly explicit exposures taken from the most unusual angles!

I know your readers will find my collection uniquely stimulating, and the issue in which they appeared would be guaranteed sold out on the first day they hit the news stands!

I shall be flying to New York on Tuesday April 30th, and will hot-foot into your Office at about 12.30 to share my exciting Portfolio with you!

I look forward to meeting you.

Yours sincerely,

Bruce de West

P.S. In the event of your considering the more unorthodox poses to be more than your readers could handle, I am sure you personally will derive great excitement from them in the privacy of your own home!

Note: No reply received. —Ed.

309-941 West 13th Avenue
Vancouver
British Columbia
Canada V5Z 1P4

McDonalds Corporation
One McDonald Plaza
Oak Brook
Illinois 60521
U.S.A.

January 3rd 1985

For the attention of Michael R. Quinlan
President

Dear Mr. Quinlan,

As a frequent consumer of your fine gourmet comestibles,
I should be intrigued to partake of luncheon at the charming
establishment which features in your many television commercials.

The Restaurant in question is certainly a most attractive
looking venue, all the staff and customers are clean, tidy and
speak good English, service is prompt and courteous, and the
general atmosphere appears most conducive to agreeable digestion.

Why is it then that all your other outlets are such a
depressing contrast to the facility described above?

On the rare occasions when the serving staff are able to
speak or understand English, one cannot make oneself heard above
the cacophony as they scurry frantically back and forth behind the
counter screaming orders at one another at maximum decibels.

When and if the order is understood, invariably it is not
cooked and a wait is inevitable, defeating the object of patronising
a fast-food emporium in the first place!

Upon eventual receipt of one's order, sitting down to consume
same is an ordeal of unhygienic forbearance, as all available
seating is occupied by elderly men who have been sitting there all
day chain-smoking cigarettes and coughing incessantly.

Should one in despair resort to the drive-through service,
one is thrown into instant confusion, as the distorted and muffled
voice barely emanating from the order speaker is completely
unintelligible, sounding like a passable impersonation of a wasp
trapped in a cardboard box!

I look forward to your divulging the whereabouts of a
McDonalds which bears any resemblance to your advertised facility.

Yours sincerely,

Bruce West

RONALD L. MARCOUX
EXECUTIVE
VICE-PRESIDENT

January 28, 1985

Mr. B. West
#309 - 941 West 13th Avenue
Vancouver, B.C.
V5Z 1P4

Dear Mr. West:

Your letter dated January 3, 1985, addressed to Mr. Michael Quinlan has been referred to me.

The restaurant shown in our advertisements is in California, constructed on a site and used for the production of television advertising. This practice is commonly used by most advertising agencies in the development of their needed creative to support the media message.

The operation of our stores is tightly controlled to maintain a very high standard of what we call, Q.S.C. & V - Quality, Service, Cleanliness and Value, and although we don't hit the oustanding mark all the time in each of the categories, we sure try our best to be the best for our customers. So far, our customers have agreed with our high operational standards because, like yourself, they keep coming back again, and again.

Drive-Thru service has been well received by our customers resulting in a very high percentage of sales recorded in the Drive-Thru window. I think your analogy of the order speaker "sounding like a passable impersonation of a wasp trapped in a cardboard box", in some cases is a good one. The ongoing work to keep these speakers up to standard with the damp climate, vandalism, etc., certainly is a challenge to say it mildly. You can be assured that, sooner or later, we will find the solution.

In conclusion, all of our stores bear the resemblance of our advertised facility from the staff through to the constructed building. I wouldn't say everything is perfect, but I can assure you we work hard at trying to make it as close to perfect as possible.

I enjoyed reading your letter, and appreciate the time you spent as a good, concerned customer, helping to make us better.

Yours truly,

McDONALD'S RESTAURANTS OF CANADA LIMITED

Ronald L. Marcoux
Executive Vice-President

RLM/kg

cc: Mike Quinlan

309-941 West 13th Avenue
Vancouver
British Columbia
Canada V5Z 1P4

C/O William Morris
151 El Camino Drive
Beverly Hills
California
90212
U.S.A.

May 22nd 1986

For the attention of Joan Collins
<u>Superstar</u>!

Dear Joan,

     I witnessed you on television last night 'acting' in one of the ubiquitously tedious soap operas, and I have to say I was startled by your amazing resemblance to my late grandmother, who passed on only three months ago!

     Even more of a coincidence, as I watched your desperately vacuous performance, I detected the unmistakable twang of a London Cockney accent, from the very same City my dear old grandparent lived all her life! I continued to watch you in some fascination, mesmerised in nostalgia as I recalled those happy childhood days in the care of my London gran!

     I expect you have lots of grandchildren of your own Joan, and I know you will sympathize with my sad bereavement this year. Just think, it could even be that you knew my granny all those years ago in London, why who knows, you might even have been in the same grade at school together!

     Would it be too much trouble to ask for a signed photo Joan? It would be a welcome treasure at this sombre time, and I thank you kindly in anticipation!

Yours sincerely,

Bruce West

Note: No reply received. --Ed.

309-941 West 13th Avenue
Vancouver
British Columbia
Canada V5Z 1P4

The Pentagon
Washington D.C.
20301
U.S.A.

May 21st 1986

For the attention of Caspar W. Weinberger
<u>Secretary of Defense</u>

Dear Mr. Weinberger,

As the U.S. Space Programme would appear to be on the brink
of lapsing into a permanent 'technical malfunction situation', I
am compelled to offer my condolences and perhaps a word of advice
here and there.

It is a cruel irony that the recent miserable failures of
Satellite Launching Rockets, the Space Shuttle, Cruise Missiles
over Alberta (Canada), etc., have overshadowed the more notable
military successes which have made America the envy of the World!

All too soon we forget the proud achievements of your
General Custer back in 1876, the defence of Pearl Harbor in 1941,
the war in Vietnam, the attempted hostage rescue in Iran under
President Carter, and of course the successful bombing of Libyan
civilians last month on the strength of Colonel Qaddafi having
conclusively been proved to have had possible connections with
terrorist attacks on European Airports.

But, I digress! My purpose in writing is to avail your
technical staff of my valuable experience in matters relating
to the problems of mechanical flight.

In my youth, I was a fanatical model aviator, and it must
be admitted that I also had my fair share of 'ongoing unscheduled
altitude loss exingency scenarios' (crashes)!

In my case, invariably it transpired that the fault was a
lack of strength and/or longevity in the Rubber-Band driving the
Propellor, and, having studied the consistency of your recent
losses, I conclude that this simple solution to your problems
might well have been overlooked by your experts?

Accordingly therefore, I enclose a Heavy-Duty Rubber-Band
for your people to test for suitability, and should this prove to
be the solution, I also enclose five dollars to purchase a good
supply of quality Bands for use on future missions!

May you soon be back on target, developing much needed
sophisticated ballistics with the necessary capacity to annihilate
as many people as possible.

                                    Yours sincerely,

                                    Bruce West

Encs.

PUBLIC AFFAIRS

12 JUN 1986

Mr. Bruce West
309-941 West 13th Avenue
Vancouver
British Columbia
Canada V5Z 194

Dear Mr. West:

We are returning under cover of this letter your check for
$5.00, made payable to Secretary of Defense Weinberger, and the
rubber band which accompanied it.

While we gratefully accept ideas and donations from citizens
who wish to improve the defense of our nation, it is indeed difficult to accept contributions from those who ridicule it. As a
result, we respectfully decline your suggestions and funds.

Sincerely,

Alice Tilton

Alice Tilton
Deputy Assistant Director
Defense Information Services Activity

Enclosures

104-1037 West Broadway
Vancouver
British Columbia
Canada V6H 1E3

C/O Peter Young
Triad Artists
10100 Santa Monica Blvd
Los Angeles
California 90067
U.S.A.

June 23 1987

For the attention of Mr. T.

Dear Mr. T.!

Hey, what's happening, man!!

So a few boring neighbors of your expensive Lake Forest home are making a hue and cry just because you single handedly desecrate a few hundred trees which weren't even on their property anyway!!!

Don't they realise who they're messing with here!!!! Mr. T.!!!!! They should count their lucky stars their own trees escaped your arboreal frenzy, and pay you for keeping them entertained in their own back-yards as well as on T.V.!!!!!!

You've certainly come a long way from your humble debut as Victoria Principal's hairdresser in 'Dynasty', to worthy acclaim as Hollywood's most respected tough-guy, and I know I'd be honored to have you living next door to me any day, Mr. T., uprooting trees and smashing the place to pieces!!!!!!!

Could you lower your chain-saw long enough to spare me a photo of you posing in your fiercest pugilistic habiliment and award-winning haircut!!!!!!!!

Thanks a bundle, Mr. T., or will you soon be changing your name to Mr. Tree!!!!!!!!!

Your biggest fan!!!!!!!!!!

Bruce West!!!!!!!!!!!

Chrysler Corporation
12000 Chrysler Drive
Highland Park
Michigan 48203
U.S.A.

104-1037 West Broadway
Vancouver
British Columbia
Canada V6H 1E3

June 8 1987

For the attention of Lee Iacocca
Chairman

Dear Mr. Iacocca,

I've just finished reading a fascinating magazine article
describing your brilliant single-handed rescue of Chrysler from
the very jaws of bankruptcy, aided only by a paltry Federal
hand-out of a billion dollars, with the result that the Corporation
now ranks as one of the most profitable automobile manufacturers
in Highland Park.

Truly this marks you as a magnate of quite exemplary stature,
Mr. Chairman, and I take my hat off to you, Sir! I've never had
to own one of your vehicles myself of course, but my chauffeur as
an ordinary working man on a limited income has owned several, and
he assures me that through his experience with Chryslers over the
years, he is steeped in admiration, at what in his considered
opinion must have been a daunting challenge!

Even more impressive, I read that notwithstanding the staggering
amount of money and energy that must have been necessary to persuade
the receptive motoring public to buy Chrysler, you also found (created?!)
time to write a best-selling Maintenance & Repair Manual, which has
sold over 73 million copies in America alone, and is <u>still</u> Number 1
in the lists!

Oddly enough, my local garage does not stock this indispensable
gem of lexical enlightenment, therefore I would be greatly obliged
if I could order a personally autographed copy in the name of my
faithful chauffeur, old Bismarck, to be sent at your earliest
convenience.

I enclose four dollars, which should be more than enough to cover
the cost of the goods and postage, and look forward to seeing this
valuable hand-book put to immediate application, upon receipt of same.

Many thanks in anticipation.

Yours sincerely,

Enc.

Bruce West

P.S. Is there any foundation to the political rumor, that you are being
      urged to run as potential Presidential candidate because the
      Federal deficit is now so serious, that by the end of next year,
      it will require the Chrysler Corporation to bail it out!

CHRYSLER MOTORS

Chrysler Motors Corporation
Service and Parts Operations

June 20, 1987

Mr. Bruce West
104-1037 West Broadway
Vancouver, Briti, CN V6H1E3

Dear Mr. West:

This will acknowledge receipt of your letter addressed to our executive offices.

Your letter was recently received at our office and has been forwarded to a more appropriate area for their attention. We appreciate your comments and believe our referral action will provide the best opportunity for review.

Thank you for writing.

Sincerely,

A. E. Pochert
Owner Relations Coordinator

/lf

Chrysler Canada Ltd.

26 South West Marine Drive,
Vancouver, B. C.
V5X 2R2

July 29, 1987.

Mr. Bruce West,
104 - 1037 W. Broadway,
VANCOUVER, B. C.
V6H 1E3

Dear Mr. West:

Your recent letter addressed to Mr. Lee Iacocca has been
reviewed and was sent to this office for reply.

I am returning your cheque for $4.00 which you sent with
your letter to cover a Maintenance & Repair Manual which was supposedly
written by Mr. Iacocca. Mr. Iacocca wrote an autobiography which
simply goes by the name "Iacocca" but to our knowledge has not written
a Maintenance & Repair Manual. His autobiography can be purchased in
any book store and of course it is available at most libraries.

Thank you for your interest and your comments.

Yours truly,

CHRYSLER CANADA LTD.,

D. C. Mallory,
Customer Relations Mgr.

DCM/vv

Attach.

Senator Gary Hart
SR-237 Russell Senate Office Building
U.S. Senate
Washington D.C.
20510
U.S.A.

4625 John Street
Vancouver
British Columbia
Canada V5V 3X4

May 8 1987

Dear Senator,

As a lifetime admirer of Democratic policy in your fine Country, I find myself watching with horror and disbelief, as the despotic Press conspires to terminate your condign bid for U.S. Presidency, through your innocent friendship with the lovely and talented young Donna Rice.

Anyone who, like myself and family, have never missed a single episode of your long-running and enchanting T.V. series, starring devoted wife, Stefanie Powers, and kindly factotem, Old Max, together with your captivating little dog, 'Freeway', who NEVER messes the carpet, must be in no doubt that any extra-marital impropriety on your part is quite unthinkable!

Yet we are lead to believe that any female unwise enough to venture into your bedroom, risks arrest by the police for loitering in a public place!

I would go further, Sir, and I mean this most fervently, when I state that if your political cogency is a reliable indication of your performance with the opposite sex, then I would have no hesitation in allowing my 23 year old Swedish-born wife to spend a night alone with you any day of the week!

But to business, Gary, we're going to have to move fast to convince the doubters out there that Donna is not the type of girl who would lead a fellow off the straight and narrow. Thus, I am prepared to lay my own reputation on the line by spending a long weekend with Donna, myself, in order to be completely satisfied that she is entirely above suspicion in her private encounters.

If you could therefore arrange our liaison at your earliest, Senator, you may rest assured that my consequent revelation to the Press will ensure a ticket to the White House in your grasp, in no time at all!

As a gesture of my sincerity, I enclose five dollars deposit, and look forward eagerly to a long weekend with Miss Rice, devoted entirely to the task of clearing your good name.

I await your early instructions.

Yours sincerely,

Bruce West

Enc.

104-1037 West Broadway
Vancouver
British Columbia
Canada V6H 1E3

Senator Gary Hart
SR-237 Russell Senate Office Building   June 22 1987
U.S. Senate
Washington D.C.
20510
U.S.A.

Dear Hart,

       Unless a positive response to my communication of
May 8 is immediately forthcoming, your name will be permanently
deleted from my Christmas Card List, without further notice.

                              Yours sincerely,

                              Bruce West

The Herald   4625 John Street
One Herald Plaza   Vancouver
Miami   British Columbia
Florida 33101   Canada V5V 3X4
U.S.A.

                                                    May 9 1987

For the attention of Heath Meriwether
<u>Editor</u>

Dear Mr. Meriwether,

        I gather, Sir, that your excellent Organ was this week solely
responsible for purging the Democratic Party of the appalling
quinquagenarian philanderer, Gary Hart.

        Excellent! Well done!!

        On behalf of all decent Christian folk in North America, I
thank you from the bottom of my heart. If the rest of the news
media practised your commendable moral responsibility, we would all
be better able to sleep at night.

        Despite your good intentions, however, it would appear that
you may have inadvertently created a new crisis for the American
voting public, for I hear on my radio this morning, that with Senator
Hart now safely dispatched, the leading Democrat for Presidential
nomination is Michael Jackson!

        Now don't misunderstand me, Michael's a fine entertainer, and
I understand he comes from an admirable religious family, but I
wonder if his background really qualifies him as White House material?

        Not that I personally subscribe to the narrow-minded view that
political experience is essential to Presidential eligibility!
After all, the faded ex-cowpuncher, Ronnie Reagan, still seems to be
holding his own, and wasn't Jimmy Carter a peanut vendor, and Richard
Nixon in the used car business?

        I should certainly appreciate your comments on this new
development, Heath, and I would also very much like to start an
immediate regular subscription to The Herald, in order to sustain
current enlightenment on important international issues.

        I await your views and subscription application, with much
interest.

                                        Yours sincerely,

                                        Bruce West

104-1037 West Broadway
Vancouver
British Columbia
Canada V6H 1E3

The Miami Herald
One Herald Plaza
Miami
Florida 33101
U.S.A.

June 22 1987

For the attention of Richard G. Capen
<u>Publisher</u>

Dear Mr. Capen,

   Is Heath Meriwether still with you?

   I wrote him on May 9, commending his excellent
work in exposing the appalling mountebank, Gary Hart, with
a request that I might be permitted a regular subscription
to your first-rate gazette, and six weeks later, I still
haven't heard from him!

   I'd be obliged if you could sort this one out
for me at your earliest, Richard.

   Many thanks.

          Yours sincerely,

          Bruce West

The Miami Herald
A KNIGHT-RIDDER NEWSPAPER

THE MIAMI HERALD PUBLISHING CO. ● 1 HERALD PLAZA, MIAMI, FLORIDA 33132-1693 ● (AREA CODE 305) 350-2111

RICHARD G. CAPEN, JR.
Chairman and Publisher
(305) 376-3525

June 26, 1987

Mr. Bruce West
104-1037 West Broadway
Vancouver, British Columbia
CANADA   V6H 1E3

Dear Mr. West:

Thank you for your June 22 letter.

No, Heath Meriwether is not the executive editor of
The Miami Herald at this time. He is now the execu-
tive editor of The Detroit Free Press, and Janet
Chusmir is The Miami Herald's new executive editor.

As you might expect, The Herald received quite a bit
of correspondence during the time of the Gary Hart
story, and it's possible that your letter got lost in
the shuffle.

I'm not quite sure I understand your question concerning a subscription to The Miami Herald. If you mean
you would like to subscribe, please let our circulation department know by either calling 305/376-3325,
or by writing to the same department at the above
address.

If you are asking for a free subscription, I'm afraid
we cannot, for obvious reasons, honor your request.
I'm returning your check to cover "postage costs."

I appreciate your comments concerning our coverage.

Sincerely,

RGC/cc
Enclosure

4625 John Street
Vancouver
British Columbia
Canada V5V 3X4

PTL Club
Heritage U.S.A.
Charlotte
North Carolina
28279
U.S.A.

May 24 1987

For the attention of Rev. Jerry Falwell

Your Reverence!

It's time to put a stop once and for all, to the treacherous
attention your praiseworthy episcopacy has attracted from the
Mephistophelean vultures that always crawl out of the woodwork
when they smell a rat at the bottom of a barrel of rotten apples!
I well remember my late Aunt Lupie constantly used to warn me that
every cloud has a bolted stable door, and we should not expect
people who live in glass houses to cast the first stone without
beating about the bush, and do you know, Your Reverence, even to
this day, I believe she was right!

Jerry, I'll come straight to the point. We have to face
facts - the PTL Club needs a new leader - a man with no traceable
record, who knows his way into the pockets of the business community,
has a red-hot sales pitch, and whose cerebration is not obstructed
by unnecessary theology!

A tall order to fill, of course, but happily the search is
over, for I'm your man! I accumulated my not inconsiderable
plunder in the house-demolition caper, which is as competitive a
business as your own, I know you'd agree? I'm temporarily side-
tracked for a short while, trying to clear the good name of Senator
Gary Hart, which seems to be taking longer than I first anticipated,
but I see no reason why I should not be able to assume my duties
with you by the end of July!

Meanwhile, it so happens that I shall be enjoying a brief
vacation in North Carolina on July 4th, and I will drop by to
tie up any loose ends regarding my appointment, at about 12.30,
for lunch. Prior to our meeting of course, Jerry, I intend to
send you a generous sum (cash!) in U.S. dollars to get things
straight before I start, and as soon as I hear from you as to the
amount appropriate to PTL Club needs, I shall remit by return!

Let's go!

Yours sincerely,

Bruce West

104-1037 West Broadway
Vancouver
British Columbia
Canada V6H 1E3

PTL Club
Heritage U.S.A.
Charlotte
North Carolina
28279
U.S.A.

June 22 1987

<u>For the attention of Rev. Jerry Falwell</u>

Dear Mr. Falwell,

    It seems ironic that every time I open a newspaper, or switch on the television, I see you pleading for funds to keep the PTL Club solvent, yet my offer of May 24, to assume administrative responsibility and donate a substantial sum of money, remains unanswered!

    Perhaps you would be good enough to let me know why your stenographic talents are so lamentably fallow, in such marked contrast to your prolific oral supplication?

Yours sincerely,

Bruce West

Jim & Tammy Bakker
688 East Vereda Sur
Palm Springs
California
U.S.A.

104-1037 West Broadway
Vancouver
British Columbia
Canada V6H 1E3

May 25 1987

Dear Jim & Tammy,

Like millions of your myopic proselytes, I have been so distressed by your untimely and iniquitous usurpation from the PTL Club, that I've been unable to put pen to check-book, or look my TV in the face since that Black Day! My sympathy is further compounded by my own recent experience as a fellow victim of cruel circumstances, which resulted in my narrowly being acquitted on a minor morals charge involving a beast of the field!

I've barely slept a wink at night lying here worrying over the terrible injustice of no longer seeing you on TV every night, Jim, in your dapper dollar-exhortation business suit, and the lovely Tammy in her super heavy duty miracle make-up, with aerodynamic Boeing-tested eyelashes palpitating to the rhythm of a thriving offertory, and now I sit in shock, watching you both waste valuable revenue time countering preposterous accusations of trivial dereliction of duty.

Jim, as you know, I have been most active in guiding Senator Gary Hart from the temptations of Satan, the recent publicity detailing this eminent wirepuller's fall from grace being well known to you of course. Regrettably my manoeuvers with the Senator have convinced me that if he is typical of the Democrat who is at large in your esteemed Country, then electoral allegiance must be firmly with the Republicans!

Sadly, with such hopeless runners as George Bush, Pat Robertson, and Robert Dole confirming everyone's worst fears that the Republicans are currently unable to field a candidate who knows how to tie his own shoelaces, there seems only one way to guarantee the successor to Mr. Reagan next year is not a Democrat, and that is for you, Jim, to forget any idea of regaining control of the PTL Club, and run as Presidential candidate for the Democrats!

With the unfortunate publicity concerning your recent activities leaving you about as popular as a headache in a nun's dormitory, it will require a great deal of money and stealth to filter you and Tammy into the political system! Happily, I am extremely wealthy, and more than willing to underwrite you in this new and exciting departure, and if you will confirm your aspiration to put your valuable experience at duping the masses to the more appropriate political application, then my financial advisers will make immediate arrangements to authorize the necessary access to my massive assets.

Praise the hoard!

Yours sincerely,

Bruce West

104-1037 West Broadway
Vancouver
British Columbia
Canada V6H 1E3

Jim & Tammy Bakker
688 East Vereda Sur
Palm Springs   June 23 1987
California
U.S.A.

Dear Jim & Tammy,

    My 'personal secretary' has brought to my attention the
disturbing news that my salutiferous offer of moral and financial
assistance dated May 25, has yet to be set in motion!

    This example of pedagogical insubordination clearly
illustrates your urgent need to take advantage of my guidance
in your future enterprises!

    Kindly let me know the score at once. Enclosed is a
dollar to cover your postal expenses.

                              Yours sincerely,

                              Bruce West

BRUCE WEST

102

June 23 19_87_

PAY TO THE ORDER OF _Jim & Tammy Bakker_ $ _1.00_

One ——————————————————————— 06/100 DOLLARS

THE ROYAL BANK OF CANADA
MAIN BRANCH - ROYAL CENTRE
1025 WEST GEORGIA STREET
VANCOUVER, B.C. V6E 3N9

MEMO

⑆102⑆ ⑈00010⑈003⑉627⑈510⑈1⑈

Dear Friend,

We inadvertently opened your correspondence addressed to the Bakkers. We are returning your contribution and apologize for any inconvenience our error may have caused you.

Jim and Tammy Bakker are no longer with the PTL Ministry so you will need to address your correspondence to them personally.

If you wish to support the ongoing work of the PTL Ministry, you will need to make your gift out to "PTL."

Thank you for understanding our situation. We hope that you will continue praying for the PTL Ministry as we strive to continue the many outreaches that are touching lives with the Gospel message.

The PTL Ministry

Her Majesty Queen Elizabeth 11
Buckingham Palace
London S.W.1.
<u>GREAT BRITAIN</u>

June 29 1987

Your Majesty,

　　　　May I take this opportunity to express my continuing
dismay over the disturbing attention the media is focusing
on your delightful and talented daughters-in-law, the Princess
of Wales, and Duchess of York?　Time was, when journalistic
treason of this excess would precipitate a timely incarceration
in The Tower, followed by beheading the perpetrators as a
final warning!

　　　　When I used to attend the Ascot races some years back,
prior to my having to leave the country at short notice, I
regret that it was never my privilege to have been approached
from the rear by the monarchy, and have one's person enjoy
sudden insertion of the Royal Umbrella, but had I been so
honored, I know I would have been very moved!

　　　　I would, if I may be permitted, Ma'am, just make one
small but important observation regarding the Princess of Wales'
reported acquaintance with the 'dashing' young banker, Philip
Dunne.　<u>Never mix with bankers</u>!　Many years back, when I was but
4 years old, my dear old white-haired Aunt Geschutz took me on
her lap, and offered immortal advice which I never forgot:
"My boy, the only time you can trust a banker is when he is
trying on a set of concrete leg-warmers at the bottom of the
ocean."

　　　　If Your Majesty would care to convey this vital
philosophy to the lovely Princess Diana with my compliments,
before it is too late, then my dear late Aunt's wise counsel
will not have been in vain.

　　　　Could you have one of the servants oblige with a
Family snapshot, Ma'am?　I would be most grateful, and offer my
humble thanks in anticipation.

　　　　　　　　　　　　　　Your ever loyal subject,

　　　　　　　　　　　　　　Bruce West

104-1037 West Broadway
Vancouver
British Columbia
Canada V6H 1E3

The University of Michigan
Presidential Selection Committee
3281C School of Business Administration
Ann Arbor   July 7 1987
Michigan 48109
U.S.A.

Dear Sirs,

        I see from your advertisement in the 'Wall Street Journal'
of June 30 that the University is in need of a President, although
I note with some surprise that no salary or benefits are mentioned?
Presumably the man appointed will have the authority to name his
own salary? Assuming this to be the case, then I am prepared to
give serious consideration to the position.

        The bulk of my academic experience has been acquired in the
formidable fields of entertainment and building demolition, which
will inevitably give me an unfair advantage over the usual crusty
no-hopers who apply for positions of this type! I am also closely
acquainted with the C.I.A. and the White House, not to mention the
Mayor of Carmel-by-the-Sea - I think this is self explanatory.

        I have an important business meeting in Detroit on July 31,
and I will drop by the University and acquaint myself with my new
surroundings and staff that day at about 12.30 for luncheon.
By then I should be in a better position to advise when I am able
to commence my duties, as by that date I should have come to a
final decision over the very attractive alternative offer I am
considering from the PTL Club management.

        Looking forward to meeting you on the 31st.

                                Yours faithfully,

                                Bruce West

P.S.   Your advertisement states that the University is "A non-
       discriminatory affirmative action employer." Very
       reassuring of course, but what on earth does it mean?
       If you are obliged to appoint everyone who applies for
       the job, would this not occasion an unnecessarily top-
       heavy management structure? Please advise.

104-1037 West Broadway
Vancouver
British Columbia
Canada V6H 1E3

Ronald Reagan Jr
C/O Mike Carlisle
1350 Avenue of the Americas
New York
N.Y. 10019
U.S.A.

June 15 1987

Dear Ronald,

It is all too easy for the ignorant critics of your recent meteoric rise to international acclaim, who are quick to ascribe your success to the notoriety of enduring a father who is President of the United States. Few members of the public can be aware of the years of dedication and personal sacrifice necessary to achieve that elusive pinnacle of accomplishment in the relentlessly competitive field of dramatic theater, a televised dance in one's underpants on 'Saturday Night Live'!

American Express' at least are surely deserving of congratulation for their astute work, in recognising your obvious talents as the perfect platform for advertising their much sought after, life saving credit cards!

But, I well remember Charlie Chaplin's son, Sydney, the Broadway stage actor, also had to cope with the stigma of having his own talents obscured by media preoccupation with his father's reputation as the world's greatest clown, and I sincerely hope you are able to overcome any such unfair comparison!

By the way, I'm a keen ballet fan, Ron, and I am delighted to be able to congratulate you on your past accomplishments in this field - a number of the fellows in my knitting circle are ex-dancers themselves, and we all regret not having had the pleasure of seeing you perform up here in Canada.

As a special gesture, if you could oblige with an autographed photo, I would be truly overwhelmed. Perhaps a shot of yourself and the great Rudolf Nureyev snapped at the climax of a pas de deux? I leave it up to you.

Thanks, Ron, you're a pal!

Yours sincerely,

Bruce West

104-1037 West Broadway
Vancouver
British Columbia
Canada V6H 1E3

The White House
Washington D.C.
20500
U.S.A.

June 25 1987

For the attention of Mrs. Nancy Reagan

Dear Mrs. Reagan,

    I hope you don't mind my writing to express my great admiration of your quite incredible energy and vitality! I saw you in that first-rate documentary 'Spitting Image' on the television recently, and I think it's just marvelous the way you staunchly support the President in his declining years! To keep the world entertained both in and out of the White House is a challenge that would exhaust most couples half your age - truly you are an inspiration to us all!

    Changing the subject briefly by the way, I keep in touch with your son (Ron Jr.) from time to time, and I should just confirm in passing that he seems to be doing fairly well, but if you have any messages for him, don't hesitate to let me know, and I will be pleased to pass them on.

    In closing, I wonder if I might presume to look to you for some rather delicate advice? A very dear friend of mine who is getting on a bit in years, is considering the pros and cons of having a facelift, but is somewhat apprehensive as she hears that after half a dozen or so operations, even an unscheduled smile can inadvertently hoist up one's tights unless extreme caution is exercised!

    Perhaps, as one of America's most glamorous and cultured personalities, Nancy, you could personally reassure my friend that this is simply not true!

    I eagerly await your cosmetic reflections, which I will convey to my friend with all dispatch.

    With grateful thanks.

Yours sincerely,

Bruce West

BRUCE WEST

105

June 25 19 87

PAY TO THE
ORDER OF Mrs. Nancy Reagan

$ 2.00

Two

00/100 DOLLARS

THE ROYAL BANK OF CANADA
MAIN BRANCH - ROYAL CENTRE
1025 WEST GEORGIA STREET
VANCOUVER, B.C. V6E 3N9

MEMO Postage costs

⑆105⑆ ⑈00010⑈003⑈627⑈510⑈1⑆

THE WHITE HOUSE

Because the White House is not authorized
to accept monetary items, we are returning
your enclosure in this envelope.

309-941 West 13th Avenue
Vancouver
British Columbia
Canada V5Z 1P4

Ann Landers
P.O. Box 11995
Chicago
Illinois 60611
U.S.A.

May 2nd 1986

Dear Ann,

I expect you're a keen movie-goer like myself, and I wonder if you saw that great film 'Arthur' with Dudley Moore and Lisa Minelli? Wasn't it funny? I really enjoyed it Ann, and I'm sure you did too.

The trouble is, ever since seeing the movie I have been plagued by a recurring nightmare, which is now getting so serious that my health is beginning to suffer. I'm too embarrassed to discuss the problem with my personal physician, so I thought I'd get your advice first, as you always come across as a sensible old broad!

The thing is, I keep dreaming that I'm having an affair with Lisa Minelli! At first I thought it was my mind temporarily playing a cruel trick on me, but now my health is seriously deteriorating, as I find it impossible to get a sound uninterrupted nights' sleep.

I've tried every sedative I can think of to stop this nocturnal torture, including hypnosis, sleeping pills, large doses of Aspirin, counting sheep, even watching 'Dynasty', but nothing prevents me from waking in a cold sweat with my heart pounding in terror every night!

Am I going out of my mind Ann?

Will this terrifying ordeal cease in due course, or do I need psychiatric attention?

Please help!

Yours desperately,

Bruce West

ANN LANDERS

May 17, 1986

Dear Bruce:

So what's wrong with a little fantasy,
dear? Perhaps if you allow yourself to get through
one dream, they will stop haunting you. It's worth
a try.

Good luck and thank you for writing.

Sincerely,

Ann Landers

AL/ms

104-1037 West Broadway
Vancouver
British Columbia
Canada V6H 1E3

The Putnam Publishing Group
200 Madison Avenue
New York
N.Y. 10016
U.S.A.

June 26 1987

For the attention of Eugene Brissie
<u>Vice President</u>

Dear Mr. Vice President,

    Word will have already reached you confirming the rumors
that my latest literary masterpiece 'Outrageously Yours' is
finally ready for publication, and I know you will be surprised
and delighted to learn that The Putnam Publishing Group has made
the short-list of houses who will be given favorable consideration
to the task of handling this remarkable Tome!

    It gives me great pleasure therefore to enclose a synopsis
of the manuscript for your favorable analysis, together with a
check for ten dollars made out to you personally, to ensure this
lucubration is submitted to the rest of your Board with your seal
of approval. If there's a problem selling it to any of the more
old-fashioned management, Eugene, let me know at once. Some of
these venerable types can be lamentably out of touch with current
business procedure, and if any dissenters need to be 'sent on
vacation' I'll make the necessary arrangements! We're both
businessmen.

    Please let my secretary know when you want me to drop over
and conclude the details of my contract, and collect the first
check in advance of royalties.

    Thanks, Gene, it's a refreshing change to be able to do
business with a man who speaks the same language!

Yours sincerely,

Bruce West

Enc.

EUGENE BRISSIE   (212) 576-8900

VICE PRESIDENT
G.P. PUTNAM'S SONS
PUBLISHER, PERIGEE BOOKS

10 July 1987

Bruce West
104-1037 West Broadway
Vancouver
British Columbia
Canada V6H 1E3

Dear Mr. West:

Thank you very much for your inquiry of June 26 concerning
your proposed book entitled OUTRAGEOUSLY YOURS. I was
indeed pleased that we were among those you chose to
review the manuscript.

Thank you also for the check for $10.00, which I very much
appreciate. Just one thing: would you please send along
another, perhaps larger, check? As a businessman, I'm
sure you'll understand.

Thank you again for your letter.

Sincerely,

E. Brissie

EB:ds

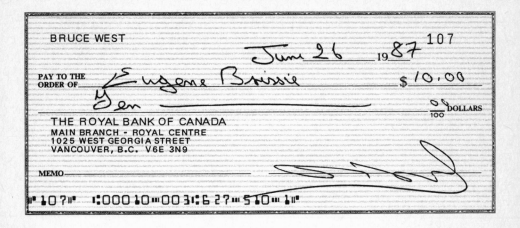

BRUCE WEST

Jun 26 19 87 107

PAY TO THE
ORDER OF   Eugene Brissie $ 10.00

Ten   00/100 DOLLARS

THE ROYAL BANK OF CANADA
MAIN BRANCH - ROYAL CENTRE
1025 WEST GEORGIA STREET
VANCOUVER, B.C. V6E 3N9

MEMO

⑈107⑈ ⑈00010⑈003⑈627⑈510⑈1⑈

104-1037 West Broadway
Vancouver
British Columbia
Canada V6H 1E3

United States Travel &
Tourism Administration
Department of Commerce
Washington D.C. 20230
U.S.A.

June 26 1987

For the attention of the Travel Director

Dear Sir,

    I am obliged to travel to your New York City in August,
in order to cement a bargain I have recently struck with a paper
trading merchant of powerful consequence in that settlement.

    I confess that I have little experience of travel in foreign
parts, and wouldst seek all guidance and favor of your valued
time in this venture, prior to departure.

    We anticipate traveling overland, unless there is now a
safe and proper railroad offering better expedition, with
essential chattels and a minimum of servants - a butler, two
assistant butlers, a waiter, an usher, two footmen, three valets,
two pages, a clerk, a messenger, a wagonmaster, an ostler,
a stable boy, a boot boy, a gamekeeper, two assistant gamekeepers,
a head steward, a housekeeper, an assistant housekeeper, a master
of the bedchamber, two bed boys, an under assistant bed boy, a
pillow boy, three maids, one handmaid, an under housemaid, a lady's
maid, a scullion, two laundress's, a charwoman, a cook, a pastry
boy, and two kitchen boys.

    I wouldst request information as to a safe trajectory free
from pestilence, warring tribesmen, and native uprising, with
details of army posts en route offering sanctuary in event of
insurgence.

    I should be pleased to submit to my physicians a separate
list of necessary inoculation against disease, and febrifuge that
should be carried on the journey. Please also be good enough to
advise on the wisdom of subjecting womenfolk to this expedition,
and detail areas where provisions and vital supplies are not
readily available, so that one may stock up at trading posts
en route.

    Your kind advice is greatly appreciated.

Yours faithfully,

Bruce West